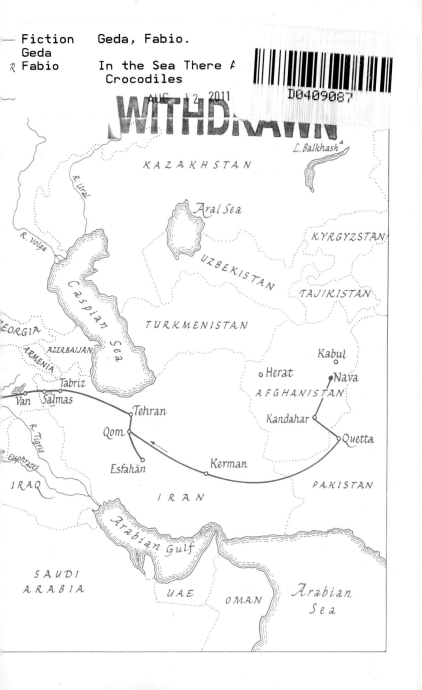

L. Balkhash

KAZAKHSTAN

R. Ural

Aral Sea

KYRGYZSTAN

R. Volga

UZBEKISTAN

TAJIKISTAN

Caspian Sea

TURKMENISTAN

EORGIA

ARMENIA   AZERBAIJAN

Kabul

Tabriz   Herat   Nava

Van   Salmas   AFGHANISTAN

R. Tigris   Tehran

Qom   Kandahar

Esfahān   Quetta

Euphrates   Kerman

IRAQ   PAKISTAN

IRAN

Arabian Gulf

SAUDI
ARABIA   Arabian
            UAE   OMAN   Sea

In the sea there are crocodiles

Fabio Geda

Translated from the Italian by Howard Curtis

In the sea
there are crocodiles

a novel

Based on the true story of Enaiatollah Akbari

DOUBLEDAY   *New York   London   Toronto   Sydney   Auckland*

Originally published in Italy as *Nel mare ci sono i coccodrilli* by B.C. Dalai
editore, Milan, in 2010. This translation first published in Great Britain by
Harvill Secker, an imprint of the Random House Group Limited, London.

www.doubleday.com

DOUBLEDAY and the portrayal of an anchor with a dolphin are registered
trademarks of Random House, Inc.

Book design by Maria Carella
Endpaper map by Reginald Piggott
Jacket illustration by Edel Rodriquez

Library of Congress Cataloging-in-Publication Data
Geda, Fabio, 1973–
[Nel mare ci sono i coccodrilli. English]
In the sea there are crocodiles : based on the true story of Enaiatollah Akbari :
a novel / by Fabio Geda ; translated by Howard Curtis. — 1st ed.
p. cm.
1. Akbari, Enaiatollah—Childhood and youth. 2. Afghanistan—
History—1989–2001—Biography. 3. Akbari, Enaiatollah—Travel.
4. Boys—Afghanistan—Biography. 5. Political refugees—Afghanistan—
Biography. 6. Afghans—Italy—Biography. 7. Political refugees—Italy—
Biography. 8. Immigrants—Italy—Biography. I. Title.
DS371.33.A32G4313 2011
305.9'06914092—dc22
[B]   2011012171

ISBN 978-0-385-53473-4

PRINTED IN THE UNITED STATES OF AMERICA

1   3   5   7   9   10   8   6   4   2

First United States Edition

Author's Note

I met Enaiatollah Akbari at a book presentation where I was speaking about my first novel, the story of a Romanian boy's life as an immigrant in Italy. Enaiatollah came up to me and said he'd had a similar experience. We got talking. And we didn't stop. I never tired of listening to his experiences, and he didn't tire of dredging them from his memory. After we'd known each other for a while, he asked me if I would write his story down, so that people who had suffered similar things could know they were not alone, and so that others might understand them better.

This book is therefore based on a true story. But, of course, Enaiatollah didn't remember it all perfectly. Together we painstakingly reconstructed his journey, looking at maps, consulting Google, trying to create a chronology for his fragmented memories. I have tried to be as true to his voice as possible, retelling the story exactly as he told it. But for all that, this book must be considered to be a work of fiction, since it is the *re-creation* of Enaiatollah's experience—a re-creation that has allowed him to take possession of his own story. At his request, the names of some of the people mentioned have been changed.

Fabio Geda, Turin 2010

In the sea there are crocodiles

Afghanistan

The thing is, I really wasn't expecting her to go. Because when you're ten years old and getting ready for bed, on a night that's just like any other night, no darker or starrier or more silent or more full of smells than usual, with the familiar sound of the muezzins calling the faithful to prayer from the tops of the minarets just like anywhere else . . . no, when you're ten years old—I say ten, although I'm not entirely sure when I was born, because there's no registry office or anything like that in Ghazni province—like I said, when you're ten years old, and your mother, before putting you to bed, takes your head and holds it against her breast for a long time, longer than usual, and says, There are three things you must never do in life, Enaiat *jan*, for any reason . . . The first is use drugs. Some of them taste good and smell good and they whisper in your ear that they'll make you feel better than

3

you could ever feel without them. Don't believe them. Promise me you won't do it.

I promise.

The second is use weapons. Even if someone hurts your feelings or damages your memories, or insults God, the earth or men, promise me you'll never pick up a gun, or a knife, or a stone, or even the wooden ladle we use for making *qhorma palaw*, if that ladle can be used to hurt someone. Promise.

I promise.

The third is cheat or steal. What's yours belongs to you, what isn't doesn't. You can earn the money you need by working, even if the work is hard. You must never cheat anyone, Enaiat *jan*, all right? You must be hospitable and tolerant to everyone. Promise me you'll do that.

I promise.

Anyway, even when your mother says things like that and then, still stroking your neck, looks up at the window and starts talking about dreams, dreams like the moon, which at night is so bright you can see to eat by it, and about wishes—how you must always have a wish in front of your eyes, like a donkey with a carrot, and how it's in trying to satisfy our wishes that we find the strength to pick ourselves up, and if you hold a wish up high, any wish, just in front of your forehead, then life will always be worth living—well, even when your mother, as she helps you get to sleep, says all these things in a strange, low voice as warming as embers, and fills the silence with words, this woman who's always been so sharp, so quick-witted in dealing with life . . . even at a time like that, it doesn't occur to you that what she's really saying is, *Khoda negahdar*, goodbye.

Just like that.

When I opened my eyes in the morning, I had a good stretch to wake myself up, then reached over to my right, feeling for the comforting presence of my mother's body. The reassuring smell of her skin always said to me, Wake up, get out of bed, come on . . . But my hand felt nothing, only the white cotton cover between my fingers. I pulled it toward me. I turned over, with my eyes wide open. I propped myself on my elbows and tried calling out, Mother. But she didn't reply and no one replied in her place. She wasn't on the mattress, she wasn't in the room where we had slept, which was still warm with bodies tossing and turning in the half-light, she wasn't in the doorway, she wasn't at the window looking out at the street filled with cars and carts and bikes, she wasn't next to the water jars or in the smokers' corner talking to someone, as she had often been during those three days.

From outside came the din of Quetta, which is much,

much noisier than my little village in Ghazni, that strip of land, houses and streams that I come from, the most beautiful place in the world (and I'm not just boasting, it's true).

Little or big.

It didn't occur to me that the reason for all that din might be because we were in a big city. I thought it was just one of the normal differences between countries, like different ways of seasoning meat. I thought the sound of Pakistan was simply different from the sound of Afghanistan, and that every country had its own sound, which depended on a whole lot of things, like what people ate and how they moved around.

Mother, I called.

No answer. So I got out from under the covers, put my shoes on, rubbed my eyes and went to find the owner of the place to ask if he'd seen her, because three days earlier, as soon as we arrived, he'd told us that no one went in or out without him noticing, which seemed odd to me, since I assumed that even he needed to sleep from time to time.

The sun cut the entrance of the *samavat* Qgazi in two. *Samavat* means "hotel." In that part of the world, they actually call those places hotels, but they're nothing like what you think of as a hotel, Fabio. The *samavat*

Qgazi wasn't so much a hotel as a warehouse for bodies and souls, a kind of left-luggage office you cram into and then wait to be packed up and sent off to Iran or Afghanistan or wherever, a place to make contact with people traffickers.

We had been in the *samavat* for three days, never going out, me playing among the cushions, Mother talking to groups of women with children, some with whole families, people she seemed to trust.

I remember that, all the time we were in Quetta, my mother kept her face and body bundled up inside a *burqa*. In our house in Nava, with my aunt or with her friends, she never wore a *burqa*. I didn't even know she had one. The first time I saw her put it on, at the border, I asked her why and she said with a smile, It's a game, Enaiat, come inside. She lifted a flap of the garment, and I slipped between her legs and under the blue fabric. It was like diving into a swimming pool, and I held my breath, even though I wasn't swimming.

Covering my eyes with my hand because of the light, I walked up to the owner, *kaka* Rahim, and apologized for bothering him. I asked about my mother, if by any chance he'd seen her go out, because nobody went in or out without him noticing, right?

Kaka Rahim was smoking a cigarette and reading a

newspaper written in English, some of it in red, some in black, without pictures. He had long lashes and his cheeks were covered with a fine down like those furry peaches you sometimes get, and next to the newspaper, on the table at the entrance, was a plate containing a pile of apricot stones, along with three succulent-looking, orange-colored fruits, still uneaten, and a handful of mulberries.

There's a lot of fruit in Quetta, Mother had told me. She had said it to entice me, because I love fruit. In Pashtun, *Quetta* means "fortified trading center" or something like that, a place where goods are exchanged: objects, lives. Quetta is the capital of Baluchistan: the fruit garden of Pakistan.

Without turning around, *kaka* Rahim blew smoke into the sun. Yes, he replied, I saw her.

I smiled. Where did she go, *kaka* Rahim? Can you tell me?

Away.

Away where?

Away.

When will she be back?

She's not coming back.

She's not coming back?

No.

What do you mean? *Kaka* Rahim, what do you mean, she's not coming back?

She's not coming back.

At that point I ran out of questions. There must have been others I could have asked, but I didn't know what they were. I stood there in silence looking at the down on *kaka* Rahim's cheeks, but without really seeing it.

It was *kaka* Rahim who spoke next. She told me to tell you something, he said.

What?

Khoda negahdar.

Is that all?

No, there was something else.

What, *kaka* Rahim?

She said not to do the three things she told you not to do.

My mother I'll just call *Mother*. My brother, *Brother*. My sister, *Sister*. But the village where we lived I won't call *village*, I'll call it Nava, which is its name and which means *gutter*, because it lies at the bottom of a narrow valley between two lines of mountains. That's why, when I came back one evening after spending the afternoon playing in the fields and Mother said, Get ready, we have to leave, and I asked her, Where? and she replied, We're leaving Afghanistan, that's why, when she said that, I thought we were just going to cross the mountains, because as far as I was concerned the whole of Afghanistan lay between those peaks. Afghanistan was those rushing streams. I had no idea how vast it was.

We took a cloth bag and filled it with a change of clothes for me and one for her and something to eat, bread and dates, and I was beside myself with excitement about the journey. I'd have liked to run and tell the others, but Mother didn't want that and kept telling me to be good and keep calm. My aunt, her sister, came over and they went off into a corner to talk. Then a man arrived, an old friend of my father's, but he didn't want to come into the house. He said we should go now, because the moon hadn't come out yet and the darkness would deceive the Taliban or whoever else we might run into.

Aren't my brother and sister coming with us, Mother?

No, they're going to stay with your aunt.

My brother's still little, he won't want to stay with my aunt.

Your sister will look after him. She's nearly fourteen. She's a woman.

But when are we coming back?

Soon.

When soon?

Soon.

I have the *buzul-bazi* tournament.

Have you seen the stars, Enaiat?

What have the stars got to do with anything?

Count them, Enaiat.

That's impossible. There are too many of them.

Then start now, said Mother. Otherwise you'll never finish.

The area where we lived, in Ghazni province, is inhabited exclusively by Hazaras, who are Afghans like me, with almond-shaped eyes and squashed noses, well, not exactly squashed, but a bit flatter than others, flatter than yours, for example, Fabio: typically Mongol features. Some people say we're descended from Genghis Khan's army. Some say our ancestors were the Koshan, the ancient inhabitants of those lands, the legendary builders of the Buddhas of Bamiyan. And some say we're slaves, and treat us like slaves.

To leave the area, or Ghazni province, was extremely dangerous for us (and I only say *was* because I don't know how things are today, though I don't suppose they've changed much), because what with the Taliban and the Pashtun, who aren't exactly the same thing but both used to treat us badly, you had to be careful who you ran into. I think that's why we left at night, the three of us: me, Mother and the man—I'll just call him the man—because Mother had asked him to go with us. We set off on foot and for three nights, under cover of darkness, with only the light of the stars to guide us—and in a place like that, without any electricity, starlight is a very powerful light—we walked to Kandahar.

I was wearing my usual gray *pirhan*: long trousers and a knee-length jacket of the same material. Mother walked in a *chador*, but she had a *burqa* in her bag to put on for when we met people, which was useful for hiding the fact that she was a Hazara, and also for hiding me.

At dawn on the morning of the first day, we stopped at one of the huts where caravans of traders break their journeys, though to judge by the bars on the windows, it must have been used for a time as a prison by the Taliban or someone. There was no one there, which was a good thing, but I was bored, so I used a bell hanging from a beam for target practice. I gathered some stones and tried to hit it from a hundred paces. I finally managed, and the man came running, grabbed me by the wrist and told me to stop.

On the second day we saw a bird of prey circling over the body of a donkey. The donkey was dead (obviously). Its legs were trapped between two rocks and it was no use to us at all because we couldn't eat it. I remember we were near Shajoi, which was one place in Afghanistan that Hazaras really had to avoid. In that area, it was said, passing Hazaras like us were captured by the Taliban and thrown alive into a deep well or fed to stray dogs. Nineteen men from my village had vanished like that on their way to Pakistan, and the brother of one of them had gone to look for him. He was the one who'd told us about the stray dogs. All he had found of his brother was his clothes, with a pile of bones inside.

That's how things are in my country.

There's a saying among the Taliban: Tajikistan for the Tajiks, Uzbekistan for the Uzbeks, and Goristan for the Hazara. That's what they say. *Gor* means "grave."

On the third day we met a whole stream of people on their way to some unknown destination, escaping from some unknown threat: men, women and children on wagons filled with hens, rolls of fabric, barrels of water and so on.

Whenever a lorry appeared going in our direction, we would ask the driver for a lift (even for a short distance). If the drivers were nice people they would stop and pick us up, whereas if they were unpleasant, or angry with themselves or at the world, they would speed up and drive past us, covering us with dust. As soon as we heard the noise of an engine behind us, Mother and I would run and hide in a ditch or among the bushes or behind some stones, if there were big enough stones. The man would stand at the side of the road and signal to the driver to stop, just like a hitchhiker, but he didn't use only his thumb, he waved his arms, to make sure they saw him and didn't run him over. If the lorry stopped and everything was safe, then he would tell us to come out of the ditch, and Mother and I would climb aboard, either in front (which happened twice) or in the back, with the merchandise (which happened once). The time we climbed in the back, the trailer was full of mattresses. I slept very well that time.

By the time we got to Kandahar, after crossing the river Arghandab, I'd counted three thousand four hundred stars (a pretty good number, I'd say) at least twenty of which were as big as peach stones, and I was very tired. Not only that. I'd also counted the number of bridges blown up by the Taliban, and the burned-out cars, and the blackened tanks abandoned by the army. But I'd still have liked to go back home, to Nava, and to play *buzulbazi* with my friends.

I stopped counting the stars when we arrived in Kandahar. I stopped because it was the first time I'd ever been in such a big city and the house lights and streetlamps would have been too distracting, even if I hadn't been too tired to keep count. Kandahar had tarred roads. There were cars and motorbikes and bicycles and shops and lots of places where men could drink *chay* and talk, and buildings as much as three storys high with aerials on the roofs, and dust, wind and dust, and so many people on the streets, there couldn't have been anybody left in the houses.

After we'd been walking for a while, the man stopped and told us to wait while he made arrangements. He didn't say where, or who with. I sat down on a low wall to count how many colored cars passed, while Mother just stood there, so still it was as if her *burqa* was empty. I could smell fried food. A radio was broadcasting news about lots of people disappearing in Bamiyán and the discovery of a large number of dead bodies in a house. An old man passed with his arms raised to the sky, crying *khodaia khair*, begging God for a bit of peace. I was starting to feel hungry, but I didn't ask for food. I was starting to feel thirsty, but I didn't ask for water.

When the man came back he was smiling, and he had another man with him. This is a good day for you, he said. This is Shaukat and he'll take you to Pakistan in his lorry.

Salaam, agha Shaukat, said Mother. Thank you.

Shaukat the Pakistani did not reply.

Go now, said the man. We'll meet again soon.

Thank you for everything, said Mother.

It was a pleasure.

Tell my sister the journey went well.

I will. Good luck, little Enaiat. *Ba omidi didar.*

He took me in his arms and kissed me on the forehead. I smiled as if to say, But of course, we'll meet again soon, take care. Then it struck me that *Good luck* and *We'll meet again soon* didn't really go together. Why wish me good luck if we were going to meet again soon?

The man left. Shaukat the Pakistani raised his hand and signaled to us to follow him. The lorry was parked in a dusty yard surrounded by a metal fence. In the back were dozens and dozens of wooden poles. Taking a closer look at them, I realized they were electricity poles.

Why are you carrying electricity poles?

Shaukat the Pakistani didn't reply.

This was something I only found out about later. Apparently, people came from Pakistan to Afghanistan to steal things: whatever there was to steal, which wasn't much. Electricity poles, for example. They came in lorries, knocked down the poles and carried them across the border, to use them or sell them, I'm not sure which. But for the moment what mattered was that we were getting a good lift, in fact, more than good, an excellent lift, because at the border they didn't check lorries from Pakistan so carefully.

It was a long journey, I couldn't tell you how long, hours and hours across the mountains, bumping along, past rocks and tents and markets. Clouds. At some point, when it was already dark, Shaukat the Pakistani got out to eat, but only him, because it was better for us if we didn't get out. You never know, he said. He brought us some leftover meat and we set off again, with the wind whistling through the window, the pane lowered just a crack to let in a bit of air but as little dust as possible. Looking at all that land rushing past us, I remember thinking about my father, because he'd also driven a lorry for a long time.

But that was different. He was forced to.

My father I'll just call *Father*. Even though he's no longer around. *Because* he's no longer around. I'll tell you his story, even though I can only tell it the way it was told to me, so I can't swear to it. What happened was that the Pashtun had forced him—not only him, but lots of Hazara men from our province—to drive to Iran and back by lorry, in order to get products to sell in their shops: blankets, fabrics, and a type of thin sponge mattress: I'm not sure what they were used for. This was because the inhabitants of Iran are Shia, like the Hazara, while the Pashtun are Sunni—it's well known that brothers in religion treat each other better—and also because the Pashtun don't speak Persian whereas we can understand it a bit.

To force him to go, they said to my father, If you don't go to Iran to get that merchandise for us, we'll kill your family, if you run away with the merchandise, we'll kill your family, if when you get back any of the merchandise is missing or spoiled, we'll kill your family, if someone cheats you, we'll kill your family. In other words, if anything at all goes wrong—we'll kill your family. Which isn't a nice way to do business, in my opinion.

I was six—maybe—when my father died.

Apparently, a gang of bandits attacked his lorry in the mountains and killed him. When the Pashtun found out that my father's lorry had been attacked and the merchandise stolen, they came to my family's house and said he'd made a mess of things, their merchandise had got lost and we had to pay them back for it.

First of all they went to see my uncle, my father's brother. They told him he was responsible now and he had to do something to compensate them. For a time, my uncle tried to find a solution, like sharing his land, or selling it, but nothing worked. Then one day he told them he didn't know what he could do to compensate them and it wasn't his business anyway, because he had his own family to think about. I don't blame him for that, because it was true.

So one evening the Pashtun came to see my mother, and said that if we didn't have money, instead of the money they would take me and my brother away with them and use us as slaves, which is something that's banned all over the world, even in Afghanistan, but that was what it amounted to. From that point on, my mother lived in fear. She told me and my brother to stay outside the house all the time, surrounded by other children, because on the evening when the Pashtun had come to our house we hadn't been there and they hadn't seen our faces.

So the two of us were always outside playing, which we didn't mind at all, and the Pashtun who passed us on the streets of the village didn't recognize us. For nighttime we had dug a hole in the fields, next to the potatoes, and whenever anyone knocked, even before going to find out who it was, we would go and hide there. But I wasn't very convinced by this strategy: I told my mother that if the Pashtun came for us at night, they certainly wouldn't bother to knock.

Things carried on like that until the day Mother decided I ought to leave because I was ten—maybe—and I was becoming too big to hide, so big that I could hardly get into the hole anymore without squashing my brother.

To leave.

I'd never have chosen to leave Nava. My village was a good place. It wasn't technologically advanced, there was no electricity. For light, we used oil lamps. But there were apples. I would see the fruit being born, the flowers opening in front of my eyes and becoming fruit. I know flowers become fruit here, too, but you don't see it happen. Stars. Lots and lots of them. The moon. I remember there were nights when, to save on oil, we ate in the open air by the light of the moon.

My house had one big room for all of us, where we slept, a room for guests, and a corner for making a fire and cooking, which was below floor level, and in winter pipes would take the heat from the fire all through the house. On the second floor there was a storeroom where we kept feed for the animals. Outside, a second kitchen, so that in summer the house didn't get even hotter than it was, and a very large courtyard with apples, cherries, pomegranates, peaches, apricots and mulberries. The walls were made of mud and very thick, more than a meter. We ate homemade yogurt, like Greek yogurt but much, much better. We had a cow and two sheep, and fields where we grew corn, which we took to the mill for grinding.

This was Nava, and I would never have chosen to leave it.

Not even when the Taliban closed the school.

Fabio, can I tell you about when the Taliban closed the school?

Of course.

You're interested?
I'm interested in everything, Enaiatollah.

I wasn't paying much attention that morning. With one ear I was listening to my teacher and, with the other, to my thoughts about the *buzul-bazi* contest we had organized for the afternoon. *Buzul-bazi* is a game played with a bone taken from a sheep's foot after it's been boiled, a bone that looks a bit like a die, although it's all lumpy, and in fact the game you play with it is a bit like dice, or like marbles. It's a game we play all year round, whereas making kites is more a spring or autumn thing, and hide-and-seek a winter game. When it gets really cold in winter, it's nice to hide among the sacks of corn or in the middle of a heap of blankets or behind two rocks, huddled up close to someone else.

The teacher was talking about numbers and teaching us to count when we heard a motorbike driving round and round the outside of the school as if looking for the front door, even though it wasn't all that difficult to find. Then we heard the engine being turned off. A huge Taliban appeared in the doorway. He had one of those long beards they all have, the kind we Hazaras can't have because we're like the Chinese or the Japanese, we don't have much facial hair. A Taliban once slapped me because

I didn't have a beard, but I was only a child and even if I'd been a Pashtun and not a Hazara I don't think I could have had a beard at that age.

The Taliban came into the classroom, carrying a rifle, and said in a loud voice that the school had to be closed immediately. The teacher asked why. My chief's orders, the man replied, you have to obey. And he left without waiting for a reply or giving any other explanation.

Our teacher didn't say anything, didn't move, just waited until the noise of the engine had petered out and then picked up the math lesson exactly where it had been interrupted, in the same calm voice and with the same shy smile on his face. Because my teacher was actually quite a shy person, he never raised his voice and when he shouted at us it was as if it hurt him more than it hurt us.

The next day the Taliban came back, the same one, riding the same motorbike. He saw that we were in class, and that our teacher was giving a lesson. He came in and asked the teacher, Why haven't you closed the school?

Because there's no reason to close it.

The reason is that Mullah Omar has given the order.

That's not a good reason.

Don't blaspheme. Mullah Omar says the Hazara schools have to be closed.

And where will our children go to school?

They won't go. School isn't for the Hazara.

This school is.

This school is against the will of God.

This school is against *your* will, you mean.

You teach things that God doesn't want taught. Lies. Things that contradict his word.

We teach the boys to be good people.

What does that mean, to be good people?

Let's sit down and talk about this.

There's no point. I'm telling you. Being a good person means serving God. We know what God wants from men, and how to serve him. You people don't.

We also teach humility.

The Taliban passed between us, breathing hard, the way I did once when I got a stone stuck up my nose. Without another word, he walked out and got back on his motorbike.

The third morning was an autumn morning, the kind when the sun is still warm, and although the first snow is blowing in the wind, it doesn't chill the air, just gives it a certain flavor: a perfect day for flying kites. We were practicing a Hazara poem in preparation for the *sherjangi*, the poetry contest, when two jeeps full of Taliban drove up. We ran to the windows to look at them. All the children in the school leaned out to have a look, even though we were afraid, because fear is seductive when you don't really know what it means.

Twenty, maybe thirty armed Taliban got out of the jeep, and the same one we'd seen twice before came into the classroom and said to the teacher, We told you to close the school. You didn't listen to us. Now *we're* going to teach *you*.

The school was a big building and there were a lot of us, maybe more than two hundred. Years earlier, when it was built, every parent had contributed a number of days' work, each person doing what he could, some making the roof, others finding ways to stop the wind coming in at the windows so we could have lessons even in winter, although they never really managed to do much about the wind: whenever we put up sheeting, the wind always tore it off. The school had several classrooms and a head-master.

The Taliban made everyone, children and adults, go outside. They ordered us to form a circle in the yard, the children in front, because we were shorter, and the adults behind. Then they made our teacher and the headmaster stand in the middle of the circle. The headmaster was pulling at the material of his jacket as if trying to tear it, and weeping and turning this way and that, looking for something he couldn't find. But our teacher was as silent as usual, his arms hanging by his sides, and his eyes open but turned inward. I remember he had beautiful eyes that dispensed goodness to everyone around him.

Ba omidi didar, boys, he said. Goodbye.

They shot him. In front of everyone.

From that day on, the school was closed, and without school, life is like ashes.

This matters a lot to me, Fabio.

What does?

Making it clear that Afghans and Taliban are different. I want people to know this. Do you know how many nationalities they were, the men who killed my teacher?

No. How many?

There were twenty of them in that jeep, right? Well, there may not have been twenty different nationalities, but almost. Some couldn't even communicate among themselves. Pakistan, Senegal, Morocco, Egypt. A lot of people think the Taliban are all Afghans, Fabio, but they aren't. Some of them are, of course, but not all of them. They're ignorant, ignorant of everything, and they stop children from studying because they're afraid those children might come to understand that they don't do what they do for God, but for themselves.

We'll say it loud and clear, Enaiat. Now where were we?

In Kandahar.

Ah, yes. Kandahar.

———

Let's get back to Kandahar.

It was morning when we left—did I already say that?—on the lorry with the electricity poles in the back. We passed through Peshawar on our way to Quetta, but Mother and I didn't get off. In Quetta we went looking for somewhere to sleep, one of those places we call *samavat* or *mosafir khama*—house of guests—with large dormitories where travelers stop on the way to Iran and look for guides for the rest of the journey. For three days, we didn't leave the place. Mother was talking to people, trying to organize her return journey, but I didn't know that. It wasn't difficult. Getting back to Afghanistan was much easier than leaving it.

In the meantime, I had nothing to do but wander around the place. Then, one night, before putting me to bed she took my head in her hands, and hugged me tight, and told me three things I shouldn't do, and that I should wish for something with all my soul. The next morning she wasn't there on the mattress with me and when I went to ask *kaka* Rahim, the owner of the *samavat* Qgazi, if he knew where she was, he told me yes, she had gone back home to be with my brother and sister. Then I sat down in a corner between two chairs, not on the chairs but on the floor, squatting on my heels, thinking that I had to think. My teacher always said thinking that you have to think is already a big step. But there weren't any thoughts in my head, only a light that swallowed everything and stopped me from seeing, like when you stare straight at the sun.

When the light went out, the streetlamps came on.

Pakistan

Khasta kofta means "as tired as a meatball," because the women where I used to live made meatballs by rolling them and rolling them and rolling them for a long time in the palms of their hands. And that was how I felt, as if a giant had taken me in his hands and made me into a meatball: my head hurt, and my arms, and another place, somewhere between my lungs and my stomach.

In Quetta there were lots and lots of Hazaras. I had seen them coming and going in and out of the *samavat* in the past few days, when Mother was still there. In fact, she'd spent a lot of time talking to them, as if she had great secrets to confide. Now I tried to approach them, but I noticed that these Hazaras were different from the ones I knew, and that even the simplest words from my country turned into complicated foreign words in their mouths because of the accent. I couldn't understand them or make myself understood, so after a while they stopped taking any notice of me and went back to their own business, which was apparently more urgent than the fact that I'd been abandoned. I couldn't ask for information or exchange a few friendly words, a few jokes that would make one of them want to help me, take me to his house, for instance, give me a cup of yogurt and a slice of cucumber. If you've only just arrived (and the fact that you've only just arrived is obvious the moment you open your mouth to ask for something), if you don't know where you are, or how things work in a place, or how you're supposed to behave, people can easily take advantage of you.

One thing I wanted to avoid (one among many others, like dying) was people taking advantage of me.

I'd shut myself up in the kitchen, but now I went to find *kaka* Rahim, the owner of the *samavat* Qgazi. He was someone I *could* communicate with, perhaps because he was used to receiving guests and so knew lots of languages. I asked if I could work there. I'd do anything, wash the floor, clean shoes, whatever needed doing. What I wanted to avoid was having to go into the street, because I was really scared. I had no idea what was out there.

He listened, though he pretended not to hear me, then said, Only for today.

Only for today? What about tomorrow?

Tomorrow you have to look for another job.

Only one day. I looked at his long lashes, the downy hairs on his cheeks, the cigarette between his teeth, the ash from which was falling on the floor, his slippers and his white *pirhan*. I thought of jumping on him, hanging on to his jacket and wailing until either my lungs or his ears burst, but I think I was right not to do it. I blessed him several times for his generosity and asked if I could take a potato and an onion from the kitchen. He said yes and I replied *tashakor*, which means "thank you."

That night I slept with my knees drawn up against my chest.

I slept with my body, but in my dreams I was awake. And I was walking in the desert.

In the morning, I woke up feeling nervous because I had to leave the *samavat* and go out onto the streets, those streets I hadn't liked at all when I'd looked out at them from the main door or from the window of the toilets on the first floor. There were so many motorbikes and cars that the air was unbreathable, and the sewer didn't run under the concrete, where you couldn't see or smell it, but between the roadway and the pavement, a few meters from the door of the *samavat*.

I went and drank some water and rinsed my face, trying to summon the courage to throw myself into the fray. Then I went to say goodbye to *kaka* Rahim.

He looked at me without seeing me. Where are you going? he said.

I'm leaving, *kaka* Rahim.

For where?

I shrugged my shoulders. I don't know, I said. I'm not familiar with the city. To be honest, I don't even know what difference it would make if I turned right or left when I got out of the door. So I'll just go to the end of the street, *kaka* Rahim, look both ways and choose the best view.

There are no views in Quetta. Only houses.

That's what I thought, *kaka* Rahim.

I've changed my mind.

About what?

I can't give you work here and pay you, pay you in money, I mean. There are too many of you. I can't give work to everyone. But you're a well-brought-up boy. So you can stay here, if you like, and eat and sleep here, until you find a place where you can really work, work and earn money and everything. But until that happens, you'll have to work hard for me from the moment you wake up until you go to sleep at night, whatever I ask you to do. Do you understand?

I smiled with all the teeth I could find in my mouth. May you live as long as a tree, *kaka* Rahim.

Khoda kana, he said.

But even though I was happy, happy and relieved, I can't pretend that everything was fine right from the start. I can't not mention that my first day working at the *samavat* Qgazi in Quetta was hell. Firstly, they immediately gave me lots of things to do. Secondly, when they asked me to do those things they didn't explain how to do them, as if I already knew everything, when in fact I didn't know anything, especially not how to do the kind of things they asked me to do. Thirdly, I didn't know anyone. Fourthly, I couldn't chat or joke with people I didn't know because I was afraid that the jokes would be misunderstood since I spoke their language very badly. Fifthly, there seemed to be no end to it. I wondered what had happened to the moon, because I didn't see it rise. I wondered if in Quetta the moon only came out from time to time, when the bosses wanted it to, in order to make people work longer hours.

By the time I went to sleep at the end of the day, I was much more than *khasta kofta*. I was feed for the hens.

I sat down on the mattress before stretching out to sleep and realized how ugly the *samavat* was: the flaking walls, the smell, the dust everywhere and, in the dust, the lice. I compared it with my house, but only for a moment, because the thought was too depressing. My instinct told me I had to forget my house. That my mother had left me here for a reason. So I waved the thought away with my hands, the way a great friend of mine, in Nava, who liked to smoke plant roots in secret, used to wave away the smoke to stop the smell clinging to his clothes.

Enaiat, Enaiat, come here, quick . . .

What is it?

Get the bucket, Enaiat. The sewer in the street is clogged up again. Bucket, rags and sticks.

What are the sticks for, *kaka* Rahim?

Bucket, rags and sticks, Enaiat. Run.

I'm running.

Enaiat, I need help.

I can't, *kaka* Zaman. The sewer is blocked, and the sewage is coming in through the door.

Again?

Again.

Lanat ba shaiton. We're always walking in shit. But the kitchen has to keep going and we're out of onions and watermelons. You have to go to the market and get them, Enaiat *jan.* As soon as you can. What's that smell?

Can you smell it, *kaka* Zaman?

What do you mean, can I smell it? It's terrible.

It's the smell of the sewage, it's coming in here.

Run, Enaiat. Rahim *agha* will be waiting for you, holding his nose.

Enaiat, where are you?

Here I am, *kaka* Rahim. Bucket and rags.

Not the new rags, stupid. The ones hanging in the yard.

I'm running, *kaka* Rahim.

Enaiat, what's happening?

The sewer, Laleh. The sewage is coming into the *samavat*.

So that's what the stink is.

I'm sorry, but I have to go and get the rags.

Come and see me after that, Enaiat, I have to ask you something.

Enaiat . . .

Yes, I'm coming, *kaka* Rahim.

I ran to get the old rags, which were hanging on a line at the far end of the yard, and the sticks. We used the rags to stop up the gap under the door, but I had no idea what the long wooden sticks were used for. I found out when *kaka* Rahim ordered me to wade into the sewage and help him push away all the stuff that had blocked the sewer. I refused, because there are certain things I'm not prepared to do. He started yelling at me, saying that if he, a grown-up in charge of an important *samavat* like the *samavat*

Qgazi, could do it, then so could I, a small child who was only there thanks to him. Yes, I replied, I was small, so small, in fact, that there were pieces of rubbish floating in the sewage that were bigger than me. In the end, other men came and helped *kaka* Rahim. But for the next few days I avoided him.

Those of us who worked in the kitchen had a room to ourselves. There were five of us, and among the five there was an elderly man I liked immediately. His name was Zaman. He was kind and gave me good advice about how not to get myself killed and how to do my work in such a way that I'd keep *kaka* Rahim happy.

In the *samavat* there were single rooms for those who had more money, big rooms for families with children, which was where I'd stayed with Mother, and the men's dormitory. I never went into the single rooms, not even later. Other people cleaned them. People came in and out constantly, speaking languages I couldn't understand. There was always smoke and noise. But I wasn't interested in all that coming and going and kept myself out of trouble.

When they saw that I wasn't someone who made a mess of things—not all the time, anyway—I started taking *chay* to the shops. The first few times I was scared of making a mistake or being swindled, but then I learned, and it became the best thing that could have happened to me. There was one place in particular that I liked: a shop that sold sandals, where every morning, about ten, I took *shir chay*, tea with milk, with *naan tandoori* made specially for *osta sahib*, the owner. The shop was close to a school.

I would go in, put the tray on the little table, greet *osta sahib* as *kaka* Rahim had taught me to, and take the money, counting it quickly, without making it too obvious that I was checking every coin, so *osta sahib* wouldn't think that I didn't trust him (it was *kaka* Rahim who had trained me to do that). Then I'd say goodbye, leave the shop and instead of going straight back to the *samavat*, I'd walk around the block until I came to the wall outside the school yard and wait for break time.

I liked it when the bell rang and the doors were flung open and the children came out into the yard, yelling and starting to play. As they played, I would imagine myself yelling and playing and calling out to my Nava friends. In my head I would call to them by their names, and kick the ball, and argue that someone had cheated in our battle to break each other's kite strings, or that it wasn't fair if I had to stay out of the *buzul-bazi* tournament for too long, just because the bone I needed was still boiling in the pot and I'd lost the old one. I walked slowly on purpose, so that I could spend more time listening to the children. I reasoned that if *kaka* Rahim saw me walking, he would probably not be as angry as if he saw me standing still.

Some mornings I was early taking the *chay* to the shop, and I would see the schoolchildren going in, all neat and clean and well combed, and I would feel bad and turn my head away. I couldn't look at them. But afterward, at break time, I liked hearing them.

You know, Enaiat, I'd never thought about that.

About what?

About the fact that hearing something is very different from looking at it. It's less painful. That's it, isn't it? You can use your imagination, and transform reality.

Yes. Or at least that's how it was for me.

I write in a room with a balcony that overlooks a primary school. Sometimes, I take a coffee break about four, and I stop and watch the parents coming to pick up their children. I watch the children coming out into the playground when the bell rings, and lining up just inside the gates, and getting up on tiptoe to peer into the crowd of adults, trying to see their parents, and the parents waving their arms when they spot them and opening their eyes and mouths wide and puffing out their chests. Everything holds its breath at that moment, even the trees and the buildings. The whole city holds its breath. Then all the questions start—how was their day, what homework do they have, how was the swimming lesson—and the mothers doing up the zips of their children's jackets to protect them from the cold and pulling their hats down over their foreheads and ears. Then everyone bundles into their cars and off they go.

Yes, I used to see them like that sometimes, too.

Can you look at them now, Enaiat?

Clothes. I had two *pirhan*. Whenever I washed one, I would wear the other and hang the wet one up to dry. Once it was dried, I would put it in a cloth bag in the corner, next to my mattress. And every evening I would check it was still there.

As the days, weeks and months passed, *kaka* Rahim realized that I was good (and again I'm not boasting), that I was good at delivering the *chay*, that I didn't drop the glasses or the terra-cotta sugar bowl, that I didn't do anything stupid like forgetting the tray in the shop, and, above all, that I always brought back all the money. And even a little more.

Because some of the shopkeepers I went to regularly, every morning about ten, and then again in the afternoon about three or four, were kind to me and gave me tips, which I could have kept for myself, but at the time I didn't know if it was right, so I handed them over to *kaka* Rahim. Not that there was much I could have done with the money. It was better that way, I think. If I'd made a mistake in counting and taken more as a tip than I should have done, *kaka* Rahim might have stopped trusting me, and I didn't want to lose a place where I could sleep and clean my teeth.

But on a day full of wind and sand, one of these shopkeepers, the *osta sahib* who sold shoes, a *sandal* or *chaplai* in my language, and who liked me, motioned me to sit down with him for a moment and have a little *chay* myself, which I wasn't at all sure I should do, but seeing that he was the one who asked me, I thought it would be impolite to refuse. I sat down on a rug on the floor, with my legs crossed.

How old are you, Enaiat?

I don't know.

More or less.

Ten.

You've been working at the *samavat* for some time now, haven't you, Enaiat?

Nearly six months, *osta sahib*.

Six months. He looked up at the sky, thinking.

42

Nobody's ever stayed that long with Rahim, he said. That means he's pleased.

Kaka Rahim never says he's pleased with me.

Affarin, he said. If he doesn't complain, Enaiat, that means he's very pleased.

I believe you, *osta sahib*.

Now I'm going to ask you a question. And you have to tell me the truth. All right?

I nodded.

Are you pleased with your work at the *samavat*?

Am I pleased that *kaka* Rahim gave me work? Of course I'm pleased.

He shook his head. No, I didn't ask if you're pleased that Rahim gave you work. Of course you are. Thanks to him you have a bed, something to eat in the evening, a cup of yogurt for lunch. I asked if you like the work. If you've ever thought of changing.

To do different work?

Yes.

What kind of work?

Selling, for example.

Selling what?

Whatever you want.

Like those boys with their wooden boxes down in the bazaar, *osta sahib*? Like them?

Like them.

I thought of it, yes. The first day. But I didn't know the language well enough. I could do it now, but I wouldn't be able to buy the merchandise.

Haven't you put any money aside?

What money?

The money Rahim pays you for your work at the *samavat*. Do you send it home or do you spend it?

Osta sahib, I don't get any money for my work at the *samavat*. Just the chance to live there.

Really?

May I be struck dead.

That skinflint Rahim doesn't even pay you half a rupee?

No.

Lanat ba shaiton. Listen, I'm going to make you a proposition. At the *samavat*, you're paid with food and a place to sleep, nothing else, but if you work for me, I'll give you money. I'll buy you the merchandise, you sell it and then we share the profit. If you make twenty rupees, I take fifteen and you take five. Your money. What do you say? You'll be able to do what you like with it.

But *kaka* Rahim won't let me sleep at the *samavat* anymore.

That's not a problem. There are plenty of places in the city where you can sleep.

Really?

Really.

I was silent for a while, then I asked *osta sahib* if I could stand up and take a walk around the block, to think it over. It was break time, and maybe the children's cries would help me find the right answer. The only thing that made me hesitate was that I was very small, as small as a wooden teaspoon. It would be easy for anyone to rob or cheat me. But in Quetta there were lots of children working on the streets, who bought merchandise wholesale and sold it again, so it wasn't as if the idea was a strange one. And then there was the fact that I'd have money of my own, which wouldn't be bad at all. True, I didn't know where I'd sleep, but *osta sahib* had said it wouldn't be a problem, and anyway all those other children had to sleep somewhere, and as for everything else—food, for instance—I could use the money I earned. And I could always go to a mosque to wash myself.

So, that morning, I didn't even have to go all the way around the block. I went back to *osta sahib* and accepted his proposition. Then I went to *kaka* Rahim and told him I was leaving and why. I thought he would lose his temper, but in fact he said I was doing the right thing and he would find another boy if he needed to. And he said that, if I ever needed something, I could come and talk to him. I really appreciated that.

————

Osta sahib and I went to a place called Sar Ab (two words that mean "head" and "water") on the outskirts of the city, to buy the merchandise.

Sar Ab is a big square filled with rusty cars and vans with their boots wide open and their owners standing next to them, each selling different things. We wandered around for a while, choosing what to buy, looking at which wholesaler was the cheapest and which had the most interesting merchandise. *Osta sahib* haggled over everything. Every single packet. He was a born trader. He bought a few snacks, some chewing gum, socks and cigarette lighters. We put everything in a cardboard box, with a string attached to it so it could be carried over your shoulder, and left. *Osta sahib* gave me quite a lot of advice. He told me who I should speak to and who I shouldn't speak to, which were the best places for selling and which weren't, what to do if the police showed up, and so on. Among all these pieces of advice, the most important was: don't let anyone steal your things.

We said goodbye and *osta sahib* raised his hand in the air and wished me good luck. It struck me that, unless there was a reserve of different pieces of good luck somewhere, to suit each occasion, this was the same good luck I had been wished by my father's old friend after he had taken us as far as Kandahar. I turned quickly and ran down the street. If I ran fast enough, I thought, someone else might get that good luck. I preferred to avoid it.

It was almost time for afternoon break at the school, and I didn't want to change my routine. I deliberately made a detour so I could stand outside the playground and hear the ball bouncing against the wall and the voices of the children chasing each other. I sat down on a low wall. When the teachers took the children back inside, I stood up and walked toward the bazaar, keeping close to the houses in order to be protected on that side, and holding the cardboard box tightly in my arms because I was really scared that something would be stolen.

The bazaar where *osta sahib* had told me to go was called the Liaqat Bazaar and it was in the center of the city.

The main street of the Liaqat Bazaar is called Shar Liaqat, and the color of that street is a combination of all the colors on the posters and signs, green, red, white, yellow, a yellow one with the words *Call Point Pco* and the telephone symbol on it, a blue one with *Rizwan Jewellers* on it, and so on, and under the English words, the Arabic words, and under the Arabic words, the dust swirling in the sunlight, and in among the dust swirling in the sunlight a swarm of people and bicycles and cars and voices and noise and smoke and smells.

In keeping with tradition, the first day was really bad, almost worse than the first day at the *samavat* Qgazi. The kind of day you want to pretend never happened, the kind of day you'd like to leave on a stone and walk away from and never see again. Obviously, I hadn't run fast enough and good luck had caught up with me.

It was evening and I hadn't yet sold anything. That could mean I wasn't any good at selling, or that nobody was interested in my things, or that everyone had already stocked up with snacks, socks and handkerchiefs, or that there was a knack to getting rid of the merchandise that I didn't know about. At that point, feeling discouraged, I leaned on a lamppost and looked at what was showing on a television in the window of a household appliance shop. I was so spellbound by some program or other—a news broadcast, a soap opera, a nature documentary, whatever it was—that I didn't notice what was happening, I swear, all I saw was a hand reach into my cardboard box, grab a packet of chewing gum and disappear.

I turned. A group of boys—six or seven of them, speaking Pashtun, probably Baluchis—were standing in the middle of the street, looking at me and laughing. One of them, who seemed to be the leader, was playing with a packet of chewing gum—my packet of chewing gum—balancing it on the back of his hand.

We started arguing, me in my language, they in theirs.

I really needed some chewing gum, the leader said.

Give it back to me, I said.

Come and get it. He made a gesture with his hand.

Should I try and get it from him? I should point out that I was a lot smaller than them and there were more of them than me and they all looked quite tough and not to be trusted. If I'd thrown myself on their leader, I'm ready to bet I would have ended up with broken bones and all my merchandise in their boxes. And what would it be like to tell *osta sahib* that everything had been stolen from me on the very first day? So, not out of fear, but rather because I'm the kind of person who thinks before doing something important, I had almost decided that it was better to lose a packet of chewing gum than my teeth, and was about to leave when—

Give it back.

Give him back the packet.

Out of nowhere, a group of Hazara boys suddenly materialized. First one, then two, then three, there seemed no end to them. Some were younger than me. They dropped from the roofs, sprang out from the back alleys. After a few minutes, there were more of us than there were of them. Seeing how things were shaping up, some of the Baluchi boys slunk away. Their leader stayed put, along with two of his followers, one on his right and one on his left, but a step behind him because they were scared. I felt as powerful as a snow leopard. With that small army behind me I approached the leader to try and get the packet of chewing gum back, but he suddenly started running. Or at least tried to. I grabbed him, and we rolled on the ground, with our boxes of merchandise and everything. I could feel his muscles under the cloth of his *pirhan*. He landed a couple of punches. As we fought I managed to grab a pair of socks from his box. Then he gave me a kick in the stomach that took my breath away, grabbed hold of his box and ran away. He still had the chewing gum. But I had the socks, which were worth more.

One of the Hazaras helped me up.

You could have joined in, I said. I wouldn't have minded.

Yes, we could, but it would have been worse for you next time. This way, you showed you could defend yourself.

Do you think so?

Yes, I do.

I shook his hand. Thanks, anyway. My name's Enaiatollah.

Sufi.

———

I made friends with the Hazara boys, and with Sufi in particular. His real name was Gioma, but he was known as Sufi because he liked to keep himself to himself, and was as calm and silent as a Sufi monk, even though there were times when he caused more trouble than anyone else.

For instance, as we were walking through the streets one evening, he went up to a vagrant lying half asleep on the ground, a dirty, smelly fellow, and dropped a handful of little stones into his metal bowl. The poor man immediately got up to see who'd given him all that money, and I'm willing to bet he was already under the illusion that he was rich and could afford a meal in the best restaurant in the city or buy himself as much opium as he wanted. That must have been why, when he realized they were only stones and saw us laughing behind the wall of a mosque, he started running after us, shouting that he'd fry us in chip oil. But we sped off, and he was too weak to catch up with us.

Another time, Sufi saw a motorbike tied to a pole and got on it. Not to steal it, just to know how it felt to be on it: he'd always dreamed of having a motorbike. But as soon as he gripped the throttle and pressed the clutch lever, for some reason the motorbike started up. It jerked forward, turning around the post it was tied to, and Sufi was thrown off and fell onto a fruit stall, hurting his back and one of his legs. For quite a while after that, he had difficulty kneeling in prayer.

Every day we went to the market with the other Hazara boys, and at lunchtime we pooled our money for a bit of Greek yogurt and chives, a few loaves of *naan tandoori*, which is a flat, round bread baked in a clay oven, and some fruit or vegetables, if there were any.

That's how it was.

I kept working at the Liaqat Bazaar because I had nothing better to do—and I would never have gone back to the *samavat* Qgazi because I'd have lost Sufi and my other friends—but I didn't like it. It wasn't like having a shop where people come in and ask you for things, and you just have to be there to welcome them and be nice. No, here you had to go up to them, stand in front of them or next to them while they were doing or thinking about other things, and say, Buy, please buy. You had to bother them like a fly, and obviously that made them angry and they treated you badly.

I didn't like bothering people. I didn't like being treated badly. But everyone (including me) is interested in staying alive, and in order to stay alive we're willing to do things we don't like.

I had even come up with a few original ideas to force people to buy, and they seemed to work. One was that I would go up to those who had a child in their arms, bite into a snack without opening it, leaving a mark on the wrapper, and while they weren't looking I would give it to the child, then say to the parents, Look, he took a bite out of this snack. He's ruined it and now you have to pay for it. Another trick was to give the child a little pinch on the arm, lightly enough not to leave a mark, so that they started crying, then I would hold out a snack and say to their parents, Here's something that'll calm your child down.

But all that went against the third thing Mother had told me not to do: *don't cheat.*

Apart from that, the big problem was where to sleep. When it got dark the boys and I would hole up in one of the more squalid neighborhoods on the outskirts of Quetta. Abandoned houses about to collapse. Drug addicts behind the cars. Fires. Garbage. I was very dirty, but every morning, even before looking for something to eat, I would go to a mosque to wash myself, and then walk past the same school as before.

I didn't skip a day. As if I felt I'd be playing truant if I did.

One afternoon I talked to *osta sahib*, the shopkeeper I'd gone into business with, and told him I wanted to quit and that I'd rather look for other work, because I couldn't stand sleeping in the street anymore.

Without saying a word, he took a piece of paper and did the accounts. Then he told me how much I'd earned so far. I couldn't believe it. He took the coins and notes and put them into my hand. It was quite a bit of money. I'd never had so much money in my life.

Then he said, If the problem is where to sleep, come to the shop in the evening, before I close up. I'll let you sleep here.

In the shop?

In the shop.

I looked around. It was a clean place, with rugs on the floor and cushions propped up against the wall. There was no water and no toilet, but there was a mosque nearby where I could go in the morning.

I accepted. In the evening, I would arrive at the shop before seven, and he would pull down the shutter. He wouldn't leave me the keys, so I had to stay in there all night until he came to open up the next day, and sometimes he didn't come until ten or later. Waiting for him to come and let me out, and having nothing else to do, I remember I tried to read the newspapers he left on the counter, but I never managed to learn Urdu well. I'd have to read slowly, so slowly that by the time I got halfway down the page, I couldn't remember what it had said at the beginning. I was looking for news about Afghanistan.

Why don't you tell me a bit more about Afghanistan before we go on?

What kind of thing?

Something about your mother, or your friends. Your relatives. Your village.

I don't want to talk about people, I don't want to talk about places. They aren't important.

Why?

Facts are important. The story is important. It's what happens to you that changes your life, not where or who with.

One winter morning—every day in winter I would look up at the sky hoping it would snow, the way it did in Nava, but although winter in Quetta was so cold it could take your skin off, it was the worst thing possible, a winter without snow: when I realized it wasn't going to snow I cried as I'd never cried up to that point—anyway, one winter morning, I went into a shop that sold plates and glasses and asked the shopkeeper for a drop of water. He looked me up and down as if I was an insect, then said, First tell me who you are. Are you Shia or Muslim? Theoretically, they're the same thing, so it was a really stupid question. I got angry. Patience has its limits even when you're a child no taller than a goat.

First I'm a Shia, I said, then I'm a Muslim. Or rather, I added, first I'm a Hazara, then a Shia, then a Muslim.

I could easily have told him I was a Muslim and left it at that, but I said what I said just to spite him. He took a broom and started beating me with the stick, very hard, without mercy. He hit me on my head and back. I ran out of the shop screaming, partly from anger and partly from pain, and the people who were there just stood around and did nothing. I bent down and picked up a stone and threw it into the shop, such a well-aimed, accurate shot that if an American had seen me he'd have immediately hired me to play on a baseball team. I didn't want to hit the shopkeeper, just break a few plates and glasses. He hid under the counter to dodge the stone and the stone shattered all the things displayed in a wooden cabinet behind him. I ran off, and never once went back to that street.

On the afternoon of the same day—I don't know where Sufi was, sometimes he went off on his own—I went to an Indian place to buy some *ash*. *Ash* is a bean soup with long thin noodles, a bit like minestrone. Anyway, I'd gone to buy *ash*—I'd earned a bit of extra money and wanted to treat myself, because I was really fed up with *naan tandoori* and Greek yogurt—and I'd just taken the bowl when one of the usual longbeards came up to me and said, Why are you eating *ash* bought from an Indian?

Now you need to know, Fabio, that eating *ash* is a sin—I don't know why, but it is—but I had already tasted the *ash*, and it was very good, I swear. And if a food is as good as that, I don't think it can be a sin to eat it, do you? So I replied, I like it, why can't I eat it?

I wasn't in an indoor restaurant, that was why the longbeard had seen me. I was in a dusty little square and in the middle of the square was the Indian with the pot. Once you'd paid for your bowl of *ash*, the Indian gave you a bowl and a spoon, and you went into a corner and ate it standing up, then gave everything back to him. You couldn't have a system like that in this country, Fabio, for hygiene reasons.

I don't know who that longbeard was exactly. He had a huge white turban on his head, so thick that even if you'd hit him a thousand times he wouldn't have felt a thing, and his mouth was covered with his beard, so that when he spoke you couldn't see his lips move, just his cheeks a little, as if he was a ventriloquist, but in all probability he was a Wahhabi, one of those fundamentalists who are always yelling about jihad and so on.

So what does he do? He takes the bowl and turns

it upside down. And I had paid for that soup: it was my soup. But all I could do was look at the soup drying on the ground and a cat eating my beans.

That's it, I thought.

I was fed up with being treated badly. I was fed up with the fundamentalists, the police who stopped you and asked you for your passport and, when you said you didn't have one, took your money and kept it for themselves. And you had to give them the money straightaway, otherwise they took you to the police station and punched and kicked you. I was fed up risking my life, like that time I was saved by a miracle from a fundamentalist attack because we boys from the Liaqat Bazaar hadn't gone to pray in the biggest Shia mosque in Quetta, as we usually did, and I'm not even sure why we didn't that day, but sometime later we heard a very loud explosion and ran to see. We were told that two suicide bombers had tried to get in. One had been stopped, but the other had succeeded. They'd both blown themselves up. Nineteen people had died inside and outside the mosque, or so I was told.

I met a lot of boys who were going to Iran. Or who had come back from Iran. They said things were better in Iran than in Pakistan (which I didn't doubt: I'd have sworn that anywhere on earth was better than Quetta) and that there was much more work in Iran. And apart from that, there was the question of religion. They were Shia—the Iranians, I mean—which was better for us Hazara, for the stupid reason that brothers in religion treat each other better, though as far as I'm concerned you should be kind to everyone and shouldn't have to check their identity card or religious affiliation.

I heard these voices in the air, as if broadcast through a loudspeaker like a muezzin's prayer, I sensed them in the flight of birds, and I believed them, because I was small, and when you're small what do you know of the world? Listening and believing were the same thing. I believed everything people told me.

So when I heard those things—that the Iranians were Shia and they treated you well and there was work— and when I saw Afghan boys in the street who'd been in Teheran or Qom and now had money in their pockets, and clean hair, and new clothes and trainers instead of slippers, whereas we Hazaras who worked at the Liaqat Bazaar stank like goats, I swear to you, when I saw these boys stop for a night at the *samavat* Qgazi, and reflected that they'd been like me once whereas now they wore jeans and shirts, I made up my mind that I would go to Iran, too.

I went back to *kaka* Rahim and asked his advice,

because of all the people I knew he was the one who knew most about traveling. Unsmiling, smoking a cigarette as usual, the smoke clinging to his long lashes, he said I was doing the right thing, going to Iran, but he said it as if doing the right thing and doing the wrong thing were the two halves of a roll which had to be eaten together, without worrying about the filling.

He wrote something on a piece of paper, a name, and handed it to me. Go and talk to him, he said. It was the name of a people trafficker and I had to introduce myself to him as a friend of *kaka* Rahim, so that he would treat me well and not be tempted to cheat me, which was something you always had to reckon with in that kind of situation. Then he went into the kitchen, put some roast chickpeas and raisins in a packet and gave it to me saying that he couldn't give me anything else, except for his blessing, his wish that I arrive safe and sound.

My mind was made up. There was no turning back.

I went to say goodbye to Zaman and promised him I would always read a bit of the Qur'an, if I happened to find a copy. I went to *osta sahib* and thanked him for everything. Then I went to find the boys in the Liaqat Bazaar and told them I was about to leave.

Where are you going?

Iran.

And how are you getting there?

With a people trafficker. I got his name from *kaka* Rahim.

If they catch you, you'll end up in Telisia or Sang Safid. Like the old madman in the market, the one with the stones in his pocket, who spends all day rubbing them because he's convinced there's gold inside them.

I was familiar with the stories circulating about Telisia and Sang Safid. Stories about beatings and abuse. I don't care, I said, I don't want to be here anymore.

They say a whole lot of people die on the border because the Iranian police shoot at you, one person said.

They say there's a lot of work, said another.

Rumors, I said. The only thing to do is go and see for myself.

Sufi was eating dates, making big chewing movements with his mouth like a camel. He wiped his mouth on the sleeve of his *pirhan*, slipped the bag from his back and put it down on the ground. With a leap backward he jumped onto a low wall, scaring away a lizard that was enjoying the sun. He was silent for a few minutes, the way he usually was, with his arms folded and his legs crossed. Then he said, Are you sure it's a good idea?

I shrugged my shoulders. I was sure of only one thing: I wanted to leave.

Ba omidi khoda. I don't want to stay here either, said Sufi.

I didn't say anything, because I was hoping he'd be the one to say it.

I'm coming with you, Enaiat.

When we went to talk to the trafficker, in a dark room filled with *taryak* smoke and a whole lot of men drinking *chay* and heating opium on camping stoves, he asked us for the money immediately. But we didn't have all the money he wanted. We emptied the pockets of our *pirhans*, turning the material inside out, gathered all the coins and crumpled notes we'd managed to save and heaped them on the table in front of him: a little hill of money.

That's all we can give you, I said. Not even half a rupee more.

He looked us up and down for a long time, as if measuring us for a suit. Your little pile of money isn't even enough to pay for a bus ticket as far as the border, he said.

Sufi and I looked at each other.

But there might be a solution, he went on, finishing cutting an apple and lifting a piece of it to his mouth with the knife. I'll take you to Iran, all right, but in Iran you'll have to work in a place I know.

Work? I said. That's fantastic. I couldn't believe my ears: not only was he taking us to Iran, he was also going to find us work.

I'll take your wages for three or four months, said the trafficker, depending on how much your journey is going to cost me. After that you'll be able to consider yourselves free and do what you like. Stay there, if you like it. Or leave, if you don't.

Sufi was so calm and silent, I half expected him to close his eyes and kneel in prayer. As for me, I was dazed by the smoke and the darkness, and was trying to think what the catch might be, because there's always a catch with traffickers, but the fact of the matter was, we didn't have any more money, and he had to pay the Baluchis and the Iranians who would get us across the border, and that was the biggest expense, so he wasn't completely wrong: we weren't his children, he didn't want to lose money on our journey. And besides, I'd introduced myself as not just anybody but a friend of *kaka* Rahim's, and that reassured me more than anything else.

Sufi and I said okay.

Be here, outside the door, tomorrow morning at eight, he said. *Khoda negahdar.*

At eight. Outside the door. But neither of us had a watch, or rather, neither of us had ever, and I mean ever, owned a watch in our lives. In Nava, to know what time it was, I measured the shadows with my steps and when there was no sun I had to guess. You woke up when it was light, and you heard the chanting of the muezzin and the crowing of the roosters. In Quetta, the noise of the city going to work would wake me, but never at a particular time. For this reason, Sufi and I had decided not to go to sleep that night.

We walked around, saying goodbye to the city.

In the morning the trafficker took us to a place about twenty minutes' walk away, where we stayed until midday and ate yogurt and cucumbers: I remember it well because it was our last lunch in Pakistan. Then we left.

First we traveled on a bus as far as the border, a bus with lots of seats. We traveled not as illegals, hidden under the seats, but with tickets like important people. We were very happy. We could never have imagined that our journey to Iran would be so comfortable, and in fact the rest wouldn't be. But we'd certainly got off to a good start.

At the border we joined another group of people. In all there were seventeen of us. We got into a Toyota pickup truck: there were four seats in front, which were taken by the trafficker and his companions, while the seventeen of us crammed into the back, packed as tightly as olives. There was even one of those longbeards—among the illegals, I mean—a fat, tousle-haired man who seemed to take an instant dislike to me, even though I hadn't done anything to him, and who during the journey tried constantly to shove me out of the truck with his knee, pretending he wasn't doing anything. After a while I had to say to him, Stop it, don't do that, don't do that, but it was like talking to a mountain, what with all the noise of the wheels and the engine. The Toyota was climbing along mountain roads, with ravines below, and even without his shoving I was already in danger of falling. I started begging him, saying I hadn't done anything wrong. Sufi didn't know what to do either, he wanted to help me, but how? At that point, without saying anything, another man, who might have been a Tajik, stood up calmly, as if he was going to go and drink a little water, punched the longbeard in the face and told him to leave me alone, because I hadn't done anything to him and we both had a long journey ahead of us and wanted to reach our destination, and there was no reason to make trouble for each other.

The longbeard calmed down.

After hours of traveling, we arrived and they made us get out. I couldn't say where we were: a low, bare, arid mountain, where the ground crunched underfoot. It was dark and there were no lights. Even the moon had hidden. The people traffickers made us hide in a cave because the order was to take only five people to the city at a time.

When it was our turn, mine and Sufi's, the traffickers made Sufi get in the back of the truck and me in the front, in the passenger seat next to the driver. They told me to squat down. Then two other people got in, so that instead of being able to look out of the window, as I'd really been hoping to do, I spent the short ride into the city between the feet of those two passengers, with the soles of their shoes resting on my back.

The city we came to, when we came to it, was called Kerman.

Iran

A two-story house. A yard with trees and a low stone wall separating it from the street, but obviously we couldn't go out there to play *buzul-bazi* or football. On the first floor there was a bathroom with a shower and two spacious living rooms with cushions and rugs and a lot of windows, all of them blacked out. The ground floor was the same. Except for the toilet, which was outside, in the yard, hidden by a cypress tree. In short, that house in Kerman was a nice house.

We and our trafficker weren't the only people there but also other groups of people, all illegals in transit, I had no idea where from. Some people were sleeping, or eating, or talking in low voices, or cutting their nails. A man was consoling a child who was lying on the floor in a corner, crying desperately. A trafficker was sitting at the table, cleaning a long knife. A lot of people were smoking and the room was shrouded in smoke. Not a single woman. Sufi and I sat down against a wall to rest. They brought us something to eat: rice with fried chicken. The rice was good, and so was the fried chicken. And maybe it was because of the fact that I was alive, in a nice house in Iran, or because of the tasty rice and fried chicken, or because of all these emotions together, but I started shaking.

I felt hot and cold at the same time. I was sweating. When I breathed, I produced a thin whistling sound, and I was shaking so much, not even an earthquake could have shaken me to the core like that.

What's the matter? said Sufi.

I don't know.

Are you ill?

I think so.

Really? In what way?

Go and call the man.

Which man?

The one who defended me from the longbeard.

The man who had stopped my bones shattering at the bottom of a ravine during the journey in the Toyota knelt down next to me, placed a hand on my forehead— his hand was so big that his fingers stretched from one ear to the other—and said, He's burning. He has a fever.

Sufi stuck a finger in his mouth. What can we do?

Nothing. He has to rest.

Could he die?

The man wrinkled his nose. *Na ba omidi khoda*, little Hazara. Who can say? Let's hope not, all right? I think he's just very tired.

Can't we call anyone, like a doctor?

They'll see to it, said the man, pointing to the Baluchis. In the meantime I'll go and get a cloth and wet it in cold water.

I remember I opened one eye. My eyelid was as heavy as the iron shutter of *osta sahib*'s sandal shop. Don't go, I said to Sufi.

I'm not going anywhere, don't worry.

The man came back with a wet cloth. He placed it gently on my forehead, and said some words I didn't understand. A few drops of water trickled through my hair and onto my neck and cheeks and behind my ears. I heard music and I think I asked something like, Who's playing? I remember the word *radio*. I remember I was in Nava, and it was snowing. I remember my mother's hand in my hair. I remember my dead teacher's kind eyes, he was reciting a poem and asking me to repeat it, but I couldn't. Then I fell asleep.

———

One after another, in small groups, everyone left the house, except for two of the traffickers. Even the nice man with the big hands left. I got a little worse, and there were several days I don't remember anything about: only a sensation of warmth and a fear of falling, of slipping away without being able to grab hold of anything. I felt so ill I couldn't move. It was as if someone had poured concrete into my arm and leg muscles. Even my veins didn't work, the blood had stopped circulating.

For a week I ate nothing but watermelon. I was very, very thirsty. If I could, I would have drunk constantly to put out the fire in my throat.

Take this.

What is it?

Open your mouth. That's right. Now drink and swallow.

What is it?

Don't sit up. Rest. *Rahat bash.*

Obviously the traffickers couldn't take me to a hospital or a doctor. That's the biggest problem about being an illegal: you're illegal even when it comes to your health. They gave me some medicines they knew, which they had in the house, little white pills to be swallowed with water. I don't know what drug it was—I wasn't only a patient, but also an Afghan and in debt to these people, so I couldn't ask any questions—but whatever it was I recovered in the end, which was all that mattered. After a week, I felt a lot better.

One morning, our trafficker told me and Sufi to get our things together—which made me laugh, because we didn't have anything to get together—and follow him.

We went to the station in Kerman.

It was the first time I had walked in a street in Iran by day, and I was starting to think that the world was much less various and mysterious than I had imagined when I was living in Nava.

The station, I remember, was a long, low building, with stone steps leading up to a row of columns under a wavy roof. And there was a sign over the roof, partly blue and partly transparent, with the words *Kerman Railway Station* on it in English, in yellow, and the same thing in Farsi, in red. Waiting for us there were two other Baluchi traffickers, partners of our own trafficker, and a small group of Afghans I had seen the day before in the house.

We got into the train through different doors. It was going nonstop to Qom. Qom is an important city between Isfahan and Teheran, a sacred place for Shia Muslims, because it houses the tomb of Fatima al-Masuma. I was in Shia territory now. And even though it didn't matter that much, I felt as if I was at home, or at least hoped I was, hoped I was in a place where I would be treated well, which amounts to the same thing.

I was euphoric.

I was cured.

I was ready and willing.

It was a wonderful sunny day, and Sufi and I were together, in Iran.

You say you felt big, Enaiat. You'd got taller because of the fever. They say children grow when they have a fever, did you know that?

Yes. I did.

How tall are you now?

One meter seventy-five, I think.

And when you were in Iran?

As tall as a child of ten or eleven. How tall are they? I don't know.

How much time had passed by then, since you'd started your journey?

Since I'd left Nava, you mean?

Yes.

Eighteen months. Yes, I'd say about eighteen months.

And we said you left at the age of ten.

That's what we said, Fabio. Although we don't know.

Although we don't know, of course.

Right.

And what time of year did you arrive in Iran?

In spring.

Good. At least time is certain.

No, Fabio. Nothing's certain.

Time is, Enaiat. It runs at the same speed in every part of the world.

Do you think so? You know something, Fabio? I wouldn't be so sure.

On the way to Qom. Speeding on a top-notch train across Iran. Seen from a distance, through the windows, Iran looked much greener than either Pakistan or Afghanistan. It was a wonderful journey, I remember: sitting comfortably, together with dozens of local passengers, the smell of eau de cologne, the dining car, clean seats soft enough to sleep in.

Our trafficker and his partners sat three or four rows from me and Sufi and all the other Afghans, so they could stay hidden among the passengers and still keep an eye on us. At the station in Kerman, before the train doors closed, they had said, Whatever happens, we don't know each other. Is that clear? You must never ever say you're with us. If the police get on the train and check you out and then tell you to follow them, do as they say. If they take you to the border, don't worry, we'll come and get you. Is that understood?

We nodded and said yes. They looked at us and asked us again if we'd understood correctly, and we said yes a second time, all in unison. Then, just to be sure and to do things properly, they asked us a third time.

I think they were a little nervous. When the ticket inspector got on, they immediately went and talked to him and showed him some papers. I think they even gave him some money.

We got off the train at Qom. For some the journey ended there—the traffickers phoned some people to come and pick them up—but Sufi and I and a few others got on a bus to take us from Qom to Isfahan. Our trafficker and the bus driver must have known each other, because when they caught sight of each other, they hugged and exchanged kisses on the cheek.

Halfway through the journey, the bus suddenly slowed down. Sufi squeezed my arm.

You're hurting me, I said.

What's going on?

I moved aside the curtains, which we'd drawn to shield ourselves from the sun. Sheep, I said.

What?

Sheep. We stopped because of a flock of sheep.

Sufi collapsed in his seat, his hands over his ears.

An hour later we arrived in Isfahan.

1) I'll take you where I want. 2) You'll work where I want. 3) For four months I'll take your wages.

Those were the conditions. Everything may have gone smoothly up until then, they may have taken care of me when I was sick, the train may have been comfortable and the coach may not have been stopped by the (Iranian) police but only by a flock of (Iranian) sheep, but now Sufi and I were going to find out where we would be spending the next four months—at least—of our lives, and what work we would be doing. That was why the journey from the bus station in Isfahan to our destination—*destination* and *destiny* are very similar, aren't they?—seemed to me longer and more dangerous, I swear, than all that getting on and off of trains and buses in the middle of nowhere that had gone before.

But when we got to a sparsely populated area on the southern outskirts of the city, our trafficker took us to a building site where they were building an apartment block, four storys high, but very, very long, with lots and lots of apartments side by side, all of them the same. There were different firms operating there, each of which had won the contract for one section. It was very hot and dusty. We walked around to the other side of the building. A tall Iranian with small eyes sprang out from behind a container filled with bricks and told us to come in.

The trafficker shook hands with the Iranian, who looked as if he must be the site foreman to judge by his clean shirt and neat beard, introduced us in a few words, just our names, as if we were expected and arrangements had been made in advance, then turned to us and said, Behave yourselves. That was all. Behave yourselves. Then he picked up his bag from the ground and left.

The site foreman scratched his head, and asked, What can you do?

Nothing, we said. (Honesty was the best policy.)

I thought as much, he replied. Come with me.

Sufi and I looked at each other and followed him.

The building was a skeleton, without doors or windows. The foreman led us to an apartment where there were no tiles on the floor, just rough, cracked concrete. This is where the people who work for us live, he said. I walked to the middle of the room and looked around. The windows and doors were sealed with nylon. There was no running water, nor any gas. The water, said the foreman, was brought by lorry, and to cook they used gas cylinders which were refilled in a nearby shop. An electric cable, patched up with adhesive tape, climbed up the outside wall of the building, came in through the window, ran along the ceiling and hung down by the door to the corridor, with a lightbulb on the end.

Go and get some sand, said the foreman. Sand. From around there.

We came back with two buckets of sand each, just to show that although we were small we were strong.

Iran

Pour it in that corner. Good, like that. Smooth it with the broom and unroll a rug on top of it. One of those over there, that's it. Unroll it. You'll sleep here until the building is finished. Then we'll go to another site. Stay clean and remember you're not alone. The better you behave, the better you'll get on with everyone, okay? You'll soon get the hang of things here, washing, eating, praying and the rest. If you have any problems talk to me, don't try and solve them yourselves. Now go down to the yard, introduce yourselves to the other workers and do what they tell you to do.

They were all illegals. Not a single one of the brick-layers, carpenters and electricians working for that firm had papers. And they all lived there, in that big housing complex, in the apartments under construction. Let's be clear about this, they didn't live in them because it made them do better work, or even work harder—although in a way both things were true: if you build a house which isn't yours, but feels like it is for the moment, you start to grow fond of it and end up taking better care of it, and if you don't have to waste time going home in the evening and coming to work in the morning, you can start work as soon as you wake up and stop just before going to bed or having dinner, if you still have the strength to eat—no, they lived there because it was the safest place to be.

The fact is, nobody ever left the site.

The site wasn't only our home.

The site was our world.

The site was our solar system.

During the first few months, neither I nor Sufi set foot outside the site. We were afraid of the Iranian police. We were afraid of ending up in Telisia or Sang Safid, and if you don't know what they are, that's only because you've never been an Afghan refugee in Iran, because all the Afghan refugees in Iran know what Telisia and Sang Safid are. They're legendary. They're supposed to be temporary detention centers, but they're more like concentration camps, judging by what I read later about concentration camps. I don't know if I'm explaining myself well. What I mean is, places without hope.

In Afghanistan, you only had to say their names to suck all the air out of a room like in those vacuum-packed bags they use for food. Clouds would cover the sun and the leaves would fall. It was said that the police there forced people to climb to the top of the hills—in those wide, open spaces—carrying a tarpaulin from a lorry on their backs, and then made them get inside the tarpaulin and rolled them down the hill onto the rocks.

When I was still in Afghanistan, I'd met two boys who'd gone mad. They talked to themselves, screamed, peed in their clothes. And I remember someone telling me they'd been in Telisia, or else in Sang Safid.

About three days after Sufi and I arrived, I saw a group of workers arguing about who was supposed to go and do something somewhere. I was running past, with a bucket in my hand, but I stopped to listen.

Go where? I asked.

To do the shopping.

To do the shopping? Outside?

Have you seen any shops on the site, Enaiat *jan*? said one of the older ones. Every week, someone has to go and do the shopping. I've been three times in the past few months. Now it's Khaled's turn. He's only been once.

Yes, but that was three weeks ago. How long is it since you last went, Hamid? Eh? How long? Two months. More than that.

That's not true. I went last month, don't you remember?

The dust has clogged up your memory, Hamid.

Anyway, the fact was that one person a week, always one of those who had been there for a long time and knew how to get around the city, did the shopping for everyone. He would take a taxi and go and buy what was needed from a particular shop, a general store where there was a bit of everything and the shopkeeper was a friend, then come straight back. Not even time for a *chay* or a bit of bread. When he came back, the shopping was divided up. We cooked together, ate together, cleaned together. Each his own task. Each his own turn.

In the end, it was the man called Hamid who went that day. I watched him get in a taxi. Good luck, *kaka* Hamid, I shouted.

Ba omidi khoda, Enaiatollah *jan*.

Watch out for the police, I said.

And you watch out for the lime. Your bag's leaking.

The lime was spilling on my shoe. I ran to the foreman. At the end of the day I stood by the gate waiting for *kaka* Hamid, and I was thinking they must have arrested him—I could already imagine him rolling down the hill at Telisia—when I saw a cloud of dust rising from around the bend and the same taxi I'd seen him getting into in the afternoon came shooting along the wall of the site and stopped in front of me. The boot was crammed full of bags. I helped him to take them out and carry them upstairs.

Thanks, Enaiatollah *jan*.

Don't mention it, *kaka* Hamid. Was everything all right? Did you see the police?

I didn't see anyone. Everything was fine.

Were you scared?

Hamid, who was piling up boxes of rice and vegetables, stopped for a second and stood there, motionless. I'm never scared, Enaiat, he said. And I'm always scared. I can't tell the difference anymore.

Did you ever visit Isfahan, Enaiat?

No.

I've heard it's very beautiful.

I looked for pictures on the Internet, once. I found lots of photos of the square named after Imam Khomeini, the Sheikh Lotf Allah mosque, and the Si-o-seh Pol bridge. I also discovered that the ruins of Bam are not far from there, with a citadel that's the largest brick structure in the world, and which was almost destroyed in an earthquake not long after I left.

They must be wonderful places.

But I didn't know that at the time. There's a saying in Iran: Esfahān nesf-e jahān, *which means: Isfahan is half of the world.*

Right. Half your world, too, Enaiat?

I have to tell the truth, because if anyone ever reads these words, any of the men I met in Isfahan, I want them to know, because I don't think I ever told them: I liked it there, on the site. So, thank you.

It's true that we worked very hard. We worked all the

time, sometimes ten or eleven hours a day. Not that there was much else to do.

As far as money was concerned, everything worked out fine. After four months the foreman stopped giving our pay to the trafficker, as agreed, and started paying us.

I remember the first wages I got: forty-two thousand *toman*.

When I'd paid my share of the monthly expenses, I had thirty-five thousand left, which was about thirty-five euros, because if I'm not mistaken, a thousand *toman* were worth one euro at that time. Those thirty-five thousand *toman* were all in notes. So, even though I was afraid, I sneaked out of the site for the first time, looking right and left and behind every corner, creeping between the houses, and went to a nearby shop and changed all the banknotes into coins, because that way I felt I had much more. I found an iron box with a padlock to keep them in. In the evening, when I finished work and went and lay down in my little corner, I would open the iron box with the padlock, take out the coins and count them—one, two, three—even though I'd already counted them a billion times. Paper money was easier to count, but coins I could pile up like towers. It was amazing.

When the money started to grow—because every month I would get my salary and there wasn't much to spend it on—and my nest egg wouldn't fit in the box anymore, I adopted a different system. I would take the notes, put them in a little plastic bag, tie it with an elastic band, nice and tight, and bury it somewhere on the site, in a place that only I knew. I wrapped the notes so they wouldn't get wet and the mice wouldn't gnaw them.

It was about that time that Sufi decided to leave. We even fell out because of it. I don't really remember how it happened, I just remember that for a while we didn't talk to each other and I felt bad about it. We might not see each other again. You never know what life has in store for you.

I'm going, he said one evening. Isfahan is too dangerous.

Where are you going?

Qom.

Why Qom? What's the difference between Qom and Isfahan?

There are lots of Afghans in Qom. They work with stones, and they're all together and everything.

He wanted to leave me. I couldn't believe my ears. You can't go, I said.

Come with me.

No. I like it here.

Then I'll go on my own.

Who told you about the Afghans in Qom? What if it isn't true?

Some boys who are working in the building for another firm. They even gave me a telephone number, look.

He showed me a piece of paper. On it was a number, written with a green felt-tip pen. I asked *kaka* Hamid for a biro and wrote down the number in an exercise book he had brought me from the shop as a gift, an exercise book with a black cover where I wrote things down so that it didn't matter if I forgot them because I had them written down. It was *kaka* Hamid who'd taught me to read and write better than I could before.

Then one morning, when I woke up, Sufi was gone.

I was starting to think that sleeping wasn't a good idea, that maybe it was better to stay awake at night, to avoid people close to me vanishing into thin air.

It's the small things that make you notice someone's absence.

I missed Sufi most at night, when I turned over in my sleep and my arms and hands didn't find him on the rug next to me. And during the day I missed him most at break time, which we used to spend together, throwing stones at jars and buckets and things like that.

One evening I finished work feeling really sad and sat down in front of the little black-and-white TV, one of those with an aerial you turn by hand, so you spend more time tuning it than watching the programs. On one channel there was a film of towers collapsing. I hopped to another channel, and they were showing the same film. A third channel: still the same film. I called *kaka* Hamid for help, and he told me it wasn't a film. That in America, in New York, two planes had crashed into the World Trade Center. They said it had been the Afghans. Then they said that it had been Bin Laden and that the Afghans were protecting him. They said it had been al-Qaeda.

I watched for a while, then had some soup and went to bed. What had happened may well have been serious, and of course I now know how serious it was, a terrible tragedy, but at that moment it seemed to me that being without Sufi was more serious.

When you don't have a family, your friends mean everything to you.

And all the while, time was passing. Seconds, minutes, hours, days, weeks. Months. My life was ticking away. I would have liked to buy a watch, just to make sense of the passing of time, a watch that showed the hours and the date and the growth of my fingers and my hair, that would tell me how much I was aging. Then the day arrived, a special day, when we stopped work on the building, because everything had been installed, even the door handles: all that remained to do was hand over the houses to their owners. So we went to work somewhere else.

We moved to a village on the outskirts of Isfahan called Baharestan. I was getting better and better at this house-building business and was often entrusted with tasks that required great expertise and responsibility (at least that's what they told me, but maybe they were making fun of me), for example, hoisting material on a rope to the upper floors of the building.

Except that, although it's true that I was getting better and everyone trusted me, I was still just as small. So what happened was, as I pulled on the rope the material got heavier than me. The load would start going down and I would start going up. Everyone laughed, and I had to shout and yell for someone to help me, shout and yell without letting go, otherwise the load would have fallen and broken and it would have been my fault.

But the best thing, what we might call my little revolution in Baharestan, was that I started leaving the site. That was because Baharestan is only a little village, and much less dangerous than Isfahan. Apart from that, I'd learned to speak Farsi* well, and lots of the people there were kind to me, especially the women.

When I saw them coming back from the shops with their bags full of shopping, I offered to carry the bags up the steps for them. They trusted me, stroked my head and sometimes gave me a sweet or something like that. I was almost starting to think that this might be a place where I could settle permanently. A place I could finally call home.

People in the area gave me a nickname: *felfeli*, which means chili pepper. The owner of a shop where I went to do the shopping, or, from time to time, to get an ice cream, always said to me *felfel nagu ce rise, bokhor bebin ce tise*, which means something like, Don't say how small the chili pepper is, but taste how spicy it is. The man was fairly elderly, and I got on well with him.

———

* A little note on the question of language, in order not to break the flow of the story. If you're not interested, just carry on reading: no one dies in the next few lines, and no information is provided that's essential to the story. The thing about language is that, at first, it was difficult for me to speak to Iranians. Their language, Farsi, is similar to Dari (which is an Eastern dialect of Farsi, spoken in Afghanistan), but the accent of Farsi isn't exactly like that of Dari. They are written in exactly the same way, but Farsi and Dari (pronounced with a stress on the last syllable: Farsī and Darī) have very different accents.

After a few months I decided to pay Sufi a visit.

Since his departure, I hadn't heard from him, but I'd had news of him from some friends who had been to his factory in Qom.

I had kept the telephone number written in the exercise book, the way you keep something precious, and one afternoon I phoned the factory. A switchboard operator replied. Sufi who? he said. There's no Sufi in our company.

Gioma, I said. Not Sufi, Gioma.

Gioma Fausi? the switchboard operator asked.

Yes, that's him.

So we said hello to each other, a bit awkwardly because it was over the phone. But although he was as calm as usual, I realized he was just as thrilled as I was.

I promised I would go and see him.

So, one hot morning, when there was hardly any wind, I took the bus to Qom. Maybe because I had been in Iran for a while and nothing had happened to me, it didn't occur to me that if I'd run into a police roadblock, my journey might have ended badly. But because it never occurred to me, everything went smoothly, as often happens when you don't think too much about things.

Sufi came to meet me at the bus station. In those months, both he and I had grown (him more than me), and we only recognized each other after giving each other the once-over at a distance for a few seconds.

Then we hugged.

I stayed in Qom for a week. He sneaked me into the factory to sleep and we went around the city and played football with the other Afghan boys. It was really nice there, but I wasn't ready to move, now that I'd found a permanent place to live. So, at the end of the week that I had taken off work, I went back to Baharestan.

Just in time to get myself repatriated.

It happened by day. We were working. I was busy preparing plaster, mixing the lime with the cement, and wasn't looking anywhere, just inside the drum of the mixer and inside myself—which is a thing I do some-times, look inside myself—and I remember I heard a car pull up, but I assumed it was the suppliers, because I knew the foreman was waiting for them.

In Iran, buildings that are side by side often have a little square in the middle which they share, a little square with only two entrances. And that helped the police. Strategically—the police are full of strategies—two cars and a van blocked one entrance, while a large number of officers walked around to the other entrance.

It was impossible to escape, and nobody tried. Those who were holding bricks and trowels put down their bricks and trowels. Those who were on their knees connecting cables for the electrical wiring let go of the cables and got to their feet. Those who were hammering nails, with the hammer in their hand and the nails in their mouths in order not to have to bend down each time to get them from the box, stopped hammering, took off their gloves, spat the nails into the sand (or just spat) and followed the policemen without a word. Not even a murmur of complaint.

Telisia. Sang Safid.

When I saw the policemen spreading out through the site and yelling, with their weapons in their hands, that was all I could think of.

Telisia. Sang Safid.

I thought of the two mad boys I'd seen in Afghanistan.

A policeman ordered me to leave everything and follow him. They herded us into the little central square, then, one at a time, led us out on the side blocked by the cars and, as soon as we were out, put us in a van.

They took hold of *kaka* Hamid, and I was afraid they would hurt him in front of us, to show what they were capable of. Instead of which they said to him, Go and get the money.

Kaka Hamid crossed the yard and went inside. We waited in silence. When he came back, he had an envelope with enough money for our return to Afghanistan. Because in Iran, when they repatriate you, it's up to you to pay for your return journey home. The State certainly won't pay for it. If they stop you in a group, as happened to us that day, you're lucky, because then the police release one of the group and tell him to go and get the money to pay for everyone's repatriation. But if they stop you when you're on your own and you have no way of paying for the journey to the border, then things turn nasty, because you're forced to stay in a temporary detention center and you have to earn the money to return home by being a slave, the slave of the center and the policemen: they make you clean up all the dirt, and I'm talking about a place which is the dirtiest place in the world, or so I've heard, a place where just to smell the fumes you'd think it was the cesspit of the earth, a place not even a cockroach would want to live.

If you don't pay, there's a risk the temporary detention center will become your home.

That day, we paid. And that wasn't all. *Kaka* Hamid told me later, in the van, that when he had gone to get the money he had found two of the boys making dinner—they hadn't noticed a thing—and asked them to stay there and look after our stuff until we came back.

Unless they took us to Telisia. Or Sang Safid.

———

Fortunately, they took us somewhere else.

They shaved our heads in the camp. To make us feel naked. And so that, afterward, people would know that we had been in Iran, as illegals, and had been expelled. They laughed as they shaved off our hair. They laughed while we stood in line like sheep. To stop myself crying, I just watched the hair piling up on the floor. It's a strange thing, hair, when it isn't on your head.

After that, they put us in lorries, and we set off at high speed. The driver seemed to be looking for potholes in the road deliberately: it was hard to believe he could hit so many without doing it on purpose. Maybe this treatment was all part of the repatriation, I thought, and I even said so to the others, but nobody laughed.

After a while they yelled at us to get out, because we had arrived. If they'd had one of those lorries for transporting sand, with a trailer that tips up, they would have tipped us out like that and let us roll onto the ground. Instead of which, they just beat us with sticks.

Herat, Afghanistan. The nearest place to the border between Afghanistan and Iran. Everyone soon made arrangements to get back to Iran, which wasn't difficult. Herat is full of traffickers waiting for people who've been repatriated. You barely have time to get beaten by the police before the traffickers pick you up and take you back.

If you don't have money with you, you can pay later. They know that if you've been working in Iran for a while you have money stashed in a hole somewhere, or that if you don't have it you can ask someone to lend it to you, without having to be enslaved for four months, the way Sufi and I were the first time. They know that.

To get back to Iran, we used another Toyota pick-up truck. But this time the journey was more dangerous, because the road was one used by smugglers for transporting illegal merchandise. Including drugs. And there were drugs on the Toyota. In Iran, if they find you with more than a kilo of opium they hang you. Of course, many policemen along the border were corrupt, fortunately, and they let you pass because you paid them, but if you happened to run into an honest one (and they did exist) then you were dead.

That time everything went well, and we got back to Baharestan.

I went straight to the site to find *kaka* Hamid, but he hadn't got back yet. My money was in its place, in the hole. The two workers who'd stayed behind had stood guard. But from that day on, everything changed. There were rumors going around that Isfahan wasn't safe anymore, and nor was Baharestan, because the police had received orders to repatriate everyone. So I called Sufi at the stonecutting factory in Qom, and he told me that, for the moment, things were quiet there.

That was when I decided to join him. I waited for *kaka* Hamid to get back, said goodbye to him, collected my things and went to the bus station.

How can you just change your life like that, Enaiat? Just say goodbye one morning?

You do it, Fabio, and that's it.

I read somewhere that the decision to emigrate comes from a need to breathe.

Yes, it's like that. And the hope of a better life is stronger than any other feeling. My mother, for example, decided it was better to know I was in danger far from her, but on the way to a different future, than to know I was in danger near her, but stuck in the same old fear.

When I got on the bus, I sat down at the back, alone, holding my bag tight between my legs. I hadn't made any arrangements with anyone—any trafficker, I mean—because I didn't want to pay money again to someone to get me to a destination where there were no problems, and after all when I'd been to Qom before, to see Sufi, everything had gone smoothly.

It was a lovely day and I curled up in my seat, my head against the window, ready to doze off.

I had bought an Iranian newspaper. I thought that if we were stopped by the police and they saw me sleeping peacefully with an Iranian newspaper on my lap, they would think I was clean. Next to me was a girl in a veil, wearing a nice perfume. Three minutes later, we left.

We were almost halfway—two women were chatting to the girl next to me, talking about a wedding they had been to, and a man was reading a book while a little boy sitting next to him, who could have been his son, was quietly singing a little song, a kind of tongue twister— we were almost halfway, like I said, when the bus slowed down and came noisily to a halt.

I thought it must be sheep. What's going on? I asked. I couldn't see anything on my side.

A roadblock, the girl replied.

Telisia. Sang Safid.

The bus driver pressed a button and the doors opened wide with a hiss. Centuries passed, the air was still, nobody spoke, not even those who had nothing to fear because they were Iranians or because their papers were in order, then the first policeman got on. He didn't seem to be in any hurry. He had one arm of his sunglasses in his hand, the other in his mouth.

When the police get on a bus, they don't ask everyone for their papers: they know perfectly well who's Iranian and who isn't. They're trained to recognize Afghans, illegals, and so on, and as soon as they see one they go straight to him and demand to see his papers even though they know perfectly well he doesn't have any.

I had to become invisible. But that wasn't one of my powers. I pretended to be asleep, because when you sleep it's as if you aren't there, and also because pretending to sleep is like pretending everything's all right and that things will work out. But this policeman was a smart one, and he saw me even though I was asleep. He tugged at my sleeve. I kept pretending to sleep and even shifted a bit in my sleep, which I tend to do during the night. The policeman kicked me in the shin. At that point I woke up.

Come with me, he said. He didn't even ask me who I was.

Where?

He didn't reply. He looked at me and put on his sunglasses, even though it was quite dark inside the bus.

I picked up my bag. I apologized to the girl next to me and asked if she could let me through, and as I passed her I got an even stronger whiff of her perfume. Everyone watched me as I walked down the aisle, and I could feel their eyes burning into the back of my neck. As soon as I stepped down onto the ground, the bus closed its doors with the same pneumatic hiss as before and set off. Without me.

There was a small police station, with a car parked outside it.

Telisia. Sang Safid.

Drums in the night.

Telisia. Sang Safid.

I can pay, I said immediately. I can pay for my repatriation. I did in fact have money with me that I'd earned on the site. But for some reason they wouldn't listen to me. One of the policemen, a huge Iranian, pushed me through a door. For a fraction of a second I imagined a torture chamber caked with blood and strewn with fragments of bone, a deep well filled with skulls, a pit going down into the bowels of the earth, little black insects crawling over the walls and acid stains on the ceiling.

What was inside?

A kitchen. That's what.

Mountains of filthy plates and pots, waiting to be washed.

Get down to work, said the huge Iranian. The sponges are over there.

It took me hours to win the battle against the remains of sauce and caked rice. I don't know how many years those pots had been there, waiting for me. As I was washing the cutlery and plates, four other Afghan boys arrived. When we'd finished in the kitchen, they took all five of us and set us to work loading and unloading cars and vans and so on. Whenever there was a boot or a trailer to be checked, the policemen called us and we started empty-ing it. When they'd finished their checking, they called us again: there were crates and suitcases to be put back, boxes to be stacked, and so on.

I stayed there for three days. Whenever I was tired, I sat down on the ground with my back against the wall and my head on my knees. If someone arrived and there was unloading and loading to be done, a policeman would come and kick us and say, Wake up, and we would get up and start again. On the evening of the third day they let me go. I don't know why. The four other boys stayed there and I never saw them again.

I got to Qom on foot.

Qom is a city with a population of at least a million—I found out later—but if you counted all the illegals in the stonecutting factories, I think the number would be double that. There are stonecutting factories everywhere. Thanks to Sufi, I started working in the same factory where he worked.

There were forty or fifty of us. They put me in the

kitchen. I made meals and did the shopping. Unlike Isfahan, in Qom I was the only one to leave the factory—in order to do the shopping—which was very, very risky for me but something I couldn't get out of.

Apart from cooking, I washed and cleaned the factory manager's office. And if there was anything else to do, like standing in for workers who were ill or moving stuff, they would call me. Ena, they would shout. Sometimes they would just call without even turning around, as if I was already there in front of them, as if I had the ability to materialize as soon as my name was uttered. In other words, I was a jack of all trades. That's what you call it, isn't it?

Whenever rocks arrived in the factory, they were cut using these huge machines, some as big as my house in Nava. The noise was incredible, and there was water everywhere. You put on boots (it was obligatory) and a plastic overall and some people even covered their ears with headphones, but with all that water on the ground and that stone dust in the air, it was difficult staying healthy and avoiding getting sick. Not just staying healthy, it was difficult staying alive. Or in one piece.

From time to time, one of the workers operating the machines, those huge machines that broke up the stones like terra-cotta and sliced through them like butter, would lose a piece of his body: an arm, a hand, a leg. We worked long hours, sometimes fourteen hours a day, and when you're tired it's easy to get distracted.

One day an Afghan boy a little bit older than me came to me and said, What's your name?

Enaiatollah.

Can you play football, Enaiatollah?

Yes, I thought, I could play football, even though I was better at *buzul-bazi*, not that I'd played it since I left Nava. Yes, I said, I can.

Really? Then be at the gate tomorrow afternoon at five. There's a tournament. We need more players.

A tournament?

Yes. Between the factories. Will you come?

Of course.

Good.

The thing is, the next day was Friday. That's important because, although life in the factory consisted of nothing but working, eating and sleeping, we did have one half-day of rest: Friday afternoon. Some people used the time to wash, and some went to see their friends. From that Friday onward, I played on the football team. We were all Afghans, as you can imagine, workers from three or four neighboring factories. There were more than two thousand Afghans working in the stonecutting factories.

I did myself proud, in those games, as far as I could.

Though sometimes I was a bit tired because my working day usually finished at ten at night.

One afternoon, after I'd been in the factory for a few months, I was lifting a really heavy stone—more than two meters long—when I lost my balance and the stone fell and shattered on the ground, with a crash you could hear all over the factory, and one sharp piece hit my foot.

It tore my trousers, sliced through my boot, scraped my calf and made a deep cut in the back of my ankle. You could see the bone. I screamed and sat down clutching my leg. One of the factory foremen came running. He told me the stone was for an important delivery, and heads would roll because it was broken. In the meantime, I was losing blood.

Get up, the man said to me.

I pointed out that I was injured.

We have to think of the stone first. Pick up the pieces. Now.

I asked if I could dress the wound.

Now, he said. But he was referring to the stone, not dressing the wound.

I started to pick everything up, hopping on one leg with the blood soaking my trousers and dripping out of the boot. I didn't even faint, just think of that. I don't know how I managed, I mightn't be able to do it today.

I finished picking up the scattered pieces, then, still hopping, went to disinfect and bandage the wound. To do that, I had to peel off a piece of flesh. I still have the scar today. And for a while I couldn't play football.

Given the gaping wound and everything, for a while I worked only in the kitchen. One day, as I was going to do the shopping, I saw a beautiful watch in a shop window. It was made of rubber and metal, and didn't cost too much. I've already said—if I'm not mistaken—that I'd often thought about having a watch, just to give some meaning to the passing of time, a watch that would show the date and tell me how much I was aging. So, when I saw that particular watch, I counted the money I had in my pocket and even though I didn't have much I realized I could buy it.

So I went in and did it. I bought the watch.

Leaving the shop, I swear, I was beside myself with joy. It was the first watch I'd ever had in my life. I kept looking at it and lifting my wrist so that I could see the sun reflected in the dial. I would have run all the way to Nava just to show it to my brother (how envious he would have been), but running all the way to Nava would have been a problem, so I ran to have it blessed at the shrine of Fatima al-Masuma, one of the holiest places in Shia Islam and one of the most appropriate (so I believed) for blessing something that means a lot to you, the way my watch did to me.

I rubbed the watch against the wall of the shrine, to purify it, but taking care not to scratch it.

I was so happy with my watch, there was a moment when I even thought that, despite the danger of losing a finger or whatever, I might stay in Qom for a long time.

Then, one night, the police came to the factory. They were well organized. They had lorries, so that they could take us straight to the border without having to go to a temporary detention center. Repatriation. Again. I couldn't believe it. It was really depressing. The police knew lots of illegals worked in that factory. They broke down the door of the shed where we were sleeping and started kicking us to wake us up.

Get your things together. We're taking you back to Afghanistan.

I was just in time to collect my things from the cabinet, with the usual envelope full of money, before they dragged me away. We paid for the repatriation, as usual. This time, though, the journey by lorry was horrible. There were so many people that those who were on the sides were in constant danger of falling out and being run over, while those in the middle were in danger of suffocating. Sweat. Breathing. Yelling. People may have even died during that journey, and nobody noticed.

We were dumped across the border, like garbage dumped on a landfill site. For a moment, I thought the thing I had never dared think: I thought of not turning back, of continuing eastward. In the east was Nava, and my mother, sister and brother. In the west was Iran, and the same old insecurity and suffering and everything else. For a moment I thought of going home. Then I recalled the words of a man I had once tried to give a letter to, a letter for my mother, when I was living in Quetta almost three years before. In the letter I asked her to come and get me. But the man had read it and said, Enaiat, I know your people's situation, I know what's happening in Ghazni province, and how the Hazaras are treated. You should consider yourself lucky to be living here. True, things aren't great, but at least you can leave home in the morning with the expectation of getting back alive in the evening. There, you never even know, when you go out, which will get back first, you or the news of your death. Here, you mix with other people and sell your things, whereas the Hazaras in your country can't even walk in the street, because if a Taliban or a Pashtun comes across them and takes a good look at them, he always finds something wrong: a beard that's too short, a turban that's not on properly, lights still on in the house after ten at night. They're in constant danger of dying for the slightest thing, being killed because of a careless word or some meaningless rule. You should be grateful to your mother that she got you out of Afghanistan, the man had said. Because there are lots of people who can't do it and who'd like to.

So I stuck my hands in my pockets, wrapped my jacket around me, and set off to find the traffickers.

But this time, at one of the roadblocks on the way back—one of the roadblocks where the traffickers paid the police to turn a blind eye—something went wrong. As well as taking the money agreed on, the police started body-searching us, looking for things to steal. What was there to steal? you may ask. You were all penniless. But even from someone who has nothing you can always take something. I had my watch, for example. It was *my* watch, and it meant more to me than anything else. Yes, of course, I could always buy another one, but it wouldn't be the same thing, it would be a *different* watch: this was my *first* watch.

A policeman made us stand in a line against a wall and passed along the line checking that we'd all emptied our pockets. Whenever he saw someone behaving oddly, or moving without permission, or making that odd kind of face—do you know what I mean?—the face of someone who has something to hide, he would go up to him and stick his nose right up against the person's face and spit out threats and pieces of his dinner, and if the threats and spitting weren't enough he'd go further and slap him or hit him with the butt of his rifle. When he reached me, he was about to walk right past me, but then he stopped and turned back and came and stood in front of me with his legs wide apart. What have you got? he asked. What are you hiding? He was thirty or forty centimeters taller than me. I looked up at him the way you look up at a mountain.

Nothing.

You're lying.

I'm not lying, *jenab sarhang.*

Do you want me to show you you're lying?

I'm not lying, *jenab sarhang.* I swear.

Well, I think you are.

Now if there's one thing I don't like, it's being hit, so, having seen him hit the others, I thought I could keep him happy somehow. I had two spare banknotes in a little pocket I'd cut in my belt. I took them out and gave them to him, hoping they'd be enough.

You have something else, haven't you? he said.

No. I don't have anything else.

He slapped me across the face, hitting my cheek and ear. I hadn't seen it coming. My cheek caught fire, my ear whistled for a few seconds. I had the impression it was swelling like a loaf of bread. You're lying, he said.

I threw myself on him, bit his cheek, tore out his hair . . . No, I showed him my wrist.

He grimaced with disappointment. To him, my watch wasn't worth anything. He angrily unfastened it from my wrist and put it in his pocket, without a second glance at me.

They let us go.

I heard them laughing in the bleak light of morning.

After that unexpected customs check, we walked for a few hours toward the nearest town, but by now it was clear that something wasn't right. Indeed it wasn't, because a police jeep suddenly appeared, its wheels sending the stones flying, and all these policemen came rushing out, yelling, Stop. We all started running. They started firing with their Kalashnikovs. As I ran, I heard the bullets whistling past me. As I ran, I thought about the kite contests on the hills of Ghazni province. As I ran, I thought about the women of Nava and how they mixed *qhorma palaw* with a wooden ladle. As I ran, I thought about how useful a hole would have been at that moment, a hole in the earth, like the one my brother and I hid in to avoid being found by the Taliban. As I ran, I thought about *osta sahib* and *kaka* Hamid and Sufi and the man with the big hands and the nice house in Kerman. And as I ran, a man running beside me was hit, at least I suppose he was, because he fell to the ground and rolled a bit and then stopped moving. In Afghanistan, I had heard lots of shooting. I could distinguish the sound of a Kalashnikov from the sound of other rifles. As I ran, I thought about which rifle was shooting in my direction. I was small. I was smaller than the bullets, I thought, and faster. I was invisible, I thought, or as insubstantial as smoke. Then, when I stopped running—because I was far enough away—I thought about leaving Iran. I'd had enough of being afraid.

That was when I made up my mind to try and get to Turkey.

Turkey

Now let's see where I was in time and in my story. I'd reached a point of no return, as you say here—because we don't say it, at least I never heard anyone say it—I was at such a point of no return that I'd even stopped remembering things, and there were whole days and weeks when I didn't think at all about my little village in Ghazni province and my mother or my brother or my sister, the way I did at the start, when their image was like a tattoo on my eyes, day and night.

Since the day I'd left, about four and a half years had passed: a year and a few months in Pakistan and three years in Iran. You have to weigh things properly, as a lady says who sells onions in the market near where I'm living now.

I was about fourteen when I decided to leave Iran: I'd had my fill of that life.

Sufi and I had gone back to Qom, after that second repatriation, but he had left a few days later, because in his opinion it had become too dangerous. He'd found work in Teheran, on a building site. Not me. I had decided to stay and work a while longer in the same stonecutting factory, to work hard and not spend any money, so that I could put enough aside to pay for the journey to Turkey. But how much did it cost to leave for Turkey? Or rather, to arrive, which was the most important thing (anyone can leave): how much would I need to spend? Sometimes, if you want to find something out, all you have to do is ask, so I asked a few friends I trusted.

Seven hundred thousand *toman*.

Seven hundred thousand *toman*?

Yes, Enaiat.

That's ten months' work, I said to a boy called Wahid, who had once thought of leaving and then hadn't. My salary at the factory is seventy thousand *toman* a month, I said. So that'll be ten months without spending even small change.

He nodded, fishing with his spoon in the chickpea soup and blowing on it in order not to burn his tongue. I also dipped my spoon in the soup. Tiny black seeds were floating forlornly on the greasy surface, along with crumbs of bread. First I moved them with the tip of the spoon, creating eddies and currents, then gathered them together, swallowed them, and finished off the soup by drinking it straight from the cup.

How to find all that money?

One afternoon, a Friday, which as I already said was our time to do what we wanted and which I spent in an endless, indeterminate—is that the right word?—football tournament against teams from the neighboring factories, anyway, one Friday this friend of mine I'd talked to at dinner about traffickers came up to the stone where I was lying with one hand on my stomach, trying to get my breath back, and asked me to listen to him for a second.

I sat up. He wasn't alone. There were other Afghans with him.

Listen, Enaiat, he said. We've talked. We want to leave for Turkey, and we've put aside enough money to pay for the journey and to pay for you, too, if you want. And we're not only doing it because you're our brother and all that, but also because when you leave with friends, the chances of everything going right are better than when you leave on your own without anyone to help you in an emergency. At that point, the team that had gone out on the field after us scored and everyone yelled for joy. What do you say? he asked after a pause.

What do I say?

Yes.

I say thank you and I accept. What else can I say?

It's a dangerous journey, you know.

I know.

Much more dangerous than the other journeys.

The ball bounced off the stone and stopped between my feet. I kicked it back with the tip of my shoe. The sun had seized every corner of the sky, the blue wasn't blue but yellow, the clouds were golden and bleeding where the mountains cut into them. The rocky peaks where stone can crush and snow can wound and suffocate.

I didn't yet know that mountains can kill.

I pulled up a blade of dry grass and started to suck on it.

I've never seen the sea, I said. There are a whole lot of things I haven't yet seen in my life and that I'd like to see. Plus, even here in Qom, it's dangerous every time I set foot outside the factory. So you know what I say? I'm ready for anything.

My voice was firm. But only because of my ignorance. If I'd known what was in store for me, I wouldn't have left. Or maybe I would. I don't know. I certainly would have said it differently.

We'd all done it. We'd all listened to the stories of those who had gone and come back. And we knew about those who hadn't made it from the accounts of their traveling companions. Maybe those companions had survived only to share their horror stories with us. It was as if the government left one or two people alive in every group to scare the others. Some had frozen to death in the mountains, some had been killed by the border police, some had drowned in the sea between the Turkish and Greek coasts.

One day, during the lunch break, I talked to a boy who had a disfigured face. Half of it looked like a McDonald's hamburger that's been left too long on the griddle.

McDonald's?

Yes, McDonald's.

It's funny. Sometimes you say things like: he was as tall as a goat. At other times, when you make comparisons, you come up with McDonald's, or baseball.

Why is that funny?

Because they belong to different cultures, different worlds. At least, that's how it seems to me.

Even if that was true, Fabio, both those worlds are inside me now.

He told me that the transit van on which he'd been traveling across Cappadocia had been involved in an accident. At a bend on an unpaved mountain road in Aksaray province, it had collided with a van loaded with lemons. He'd been thrown out and had scraped his face on the ground. Then the Turkish police had arrested him and beaten him up. And then they handed him over to the Iranians, and they'd beaten him up, too. So his journey to Europe (he wanted to get to Sweden) had turned into a bloody mess, along with his dreams. I'd lend you the money to leave, he said, but I can't because I don't want to be responsible for your pain. And there were others who said the same as him, but I'm not sure they were genuine, they might just have been skinflints.

And yet all I needed was one story that ended well. All I needed to hear was, He made it, he got to Turkey, or Greece, or London, and I immediately felt encouraged. If he had made it, I thought, then so could I.

In the end there were four of us who'd made up our minds to leave. Then we found out that Farid, a boy who was working in a factory around the corner from ours, was also planning to leave Qom. But that wasn't all. The trafficker he was going to use was his cousin.

This sounded like an opportunity not to be missed. If the trafficker really was his cousin we could trust him, and if he left with us, we would become friends of the cousin and be treated accordingly.

One day, a day like any other, we finished our shift,

put our things in canvas rucksacks, said goodbye to the manager of the factory, asked for the wages due to us and (risking the usual roadblocks) took a scheduled bus to Teheran. At the station, we found our friend's cousin waiting for us. He took us to his house in a taxi, one of those collective taxis with a lot of people inside.

In the dining room, over a cup of *chay*, he told us we had two days to get some food for the journey—simple but nutritious food, like dried fruit, almonds, pistachios—and buy a pair of heavy mountain shoes and warm, waterproof clothes. They have to be waterproof, he said. And also nice clothes to wear in Istanbul. We certainly couldn't walk around the city wearing the same clothes we'd been wearing during the journey, which would be torn and smelly by then. We had to buy all that, but especially the shoes. Our friend's cousin was really insistent about that.

So we went around the bazaars doing our shopping, and there was a euphoria in the air that I can't describe. When we got back, we showed the shoes to the trafficker to know if they were all right. He lifted them, checked the seams, bent the soles, looked inside them and everything, and said yes, they were fine.

It wasn't true.

He said it in good faith—I'm certain of that, because of his cousin—and the reason he said it in good faith was because he thought he knew what our trek across the mountains would be like, but he didn't know at all, because he'd never been there. He just had to hand us over to others. He was a go-between. He was the person we had to phone once we got to Turkey and say, We've arrived. So that the friends in Qom we'd left the money with could hand it over to him.

Holding the shoes up to the light coming in through the window, he said, Your journey will last three days. These are solid shoes, just what you need. You've done well. Excellent purchase.

The following morning an Iranian picked us up in a taxi and took us to a house outside the city, where we waited. After an hour, a bus arrived. The driver was an accomplice, and the passengers had no idea what was going on. The driver tooted his horn and we ran out of the house and climbed on the bus. The passengers— mostly women and children but also some men—looked on in astonishment. The men tried to protest, but were immediately silenced.

We set off for Tabriz (I know because I asked). We were on our way to the border, and once past Tabriz we drove along the shores of Lake Urmia which, for those who don't know, is in the middle of Iranian Azerbaijan, just to give you some idea, and is the largest lake in the country:

at its fullest, about a hundred and forty kilometers long and fifty-five wide.

I'd almost dozed off when one of my traveling companions nudged me with his elbow and said, Look.

What? I said, without opening my eyes.

The lake. Look at the lake.

I turned my head and slowly opened one eyelid, with my hands between my legs. I looked out of the window. It was sunset and the sun was low over the water. We could see dozens and dozens of rocky little islands against the light and, all over the islands, both on the ground and in the air, dots. Thousands of dots.

What are they?

Birds.

Birds?

Migrating birds, the man sitting in front told me.

Is it true they are birds, *agha sahib*? I asked the man, tapping him on the shoulder.

Flamingos, pelicans and lots of other species, the man said. Hulagu Khan, grandson of Genghis Khan and conqueror of Baghdad, is buried on one of those islands. So there are birds and ghosts. That may be why there are no fish in the lake.

No fish?

Not a single one. Bad waters. Only good for rheumatism.

It was dark by the time we got to Salmas, the last city in Iran and the closest to the mountains. They made us get out, told us to stay close together and keep quiet, and we started walking, without torches or anything.

Early in the morning, in the silence and the pale light of dawn, we came to a little village.

There was a little house that we went into as if it belonged to us, though it didn't, it belonged to a family. It was a kind of collection point for illegals who wanted to cross the mountains. A small group was already there, and soon afterward more arrived. Afghans. In the end there were thirty of us. We were scared. We wondered how so many of us would be able to cross the mountains without being seen. We asked, but didn't get an answer, and when we insisted they made it clear it was best to stop right there with our questions. We stayed in that house for two days, waiting.

Then, at sunset on the evening of the second day, they told us to get ready. We set off under a starry sky and a big moon, so we didn't need lights or torches or eyes like an owl's. We could see very well. We walked for half an hour between the fields along little paths invisible to those who didn't know them. As we reached the top of the first slope, a group of people emerged from behind a big rock. We took fright, and some yelled that they were soldiers. But they weren't, they were thirty more illegals.

We couldn't believe our eyes. Now there were sixty of us, sixty in a line on the mountain paths. But it wasn't over. Half an hour later, another group appeared. They had been squatting on the ground waiting for our arrival. By the time we were finally able to make a head count, during a brief stop in the middle of the night, there were seventy-seven of us.

They split us into ethnic groups.

Apart from the Afghans, who were the youngest, there were Kurds, Pakistanis, Iraqis and a few Bengalis.

They split us up to avoid problems, insofar as that was possible, given that we were walking all day shoulder to shoulder, elbow to elbow, with different strides, but at the same speed, and when you're in a situation like that, making a lot of effort in uncomfortable circumstances, with not much food and not much water and nowhere to rest and it's very, very cold, then squabbles and brawls and even knife fights are always in the cards, so it's best to keep the hostile ethnic groups apart.

After an hour spent walking along a very rough dirt path, we were stopped halfway up a hill by a shepherd accompanied by a dog madly chasing his own tail—the dog, not the shepherd. He asked to speak to the leader of the expedition, who without a second thought took some money from his jacket and paid him to stop him giving us away to the police. The shepherd counted the money slowly, very slowly, then put it inside his hat and signaled to us to continue.

As I passed him, the old man looked me straight in the eyes, as if to tell me something. But I didn't know what.

By night we walked.

By day we slept. Or tried to.

At the end of the third day, because the trafficker back in Teheran, our cousin's friend, had told us the journey would last three days and three nights, we wanted to know how much longer it would be before we got to the top of the mountain—to us it still seemed to be as far as ever—and started descending toward Turkey, but we were all too scared to ask any questions, so we drew lots, and I was the one picked out.

I approached one of the smugglers and said, *Agha*, please, how long is it before we get to the top of the mountain?

Without looking at me, he replied, A few hours.

I went back to my friends and said, A few hours.

We walked until just before dawn, then stopped. The muscles of our legs were as hard as concrete.

At sunset, as usual, we set off again.

He lied to you, said Farid.

I already realized that, I said, thanks. But your cousin

wasn't very accurate either when he told us how long it would take.

You have to ask someone else.

After half an hour I approached another of the Iranians, who had a Kalashnikov across his shoulder. *Agha*, please, I said, falling into step beside him, how long is it before we get to the top of the mountain?

Not long, he replied, without even looking at me.

What does "not long" mean, *agha*?

Before dawn.

I went back to my friends and said, It won't be long, if we keep up a good pace we'll get there before dawn.

They all smiled, but nobody said anything. Any strength we might have had to speak had drained out of us through our feet and our noses and hung in the clouds of steam that materialized in front of our lips. We trudged on until the sun came up over in the direction of Nava, my home. The top of the mountain was there, one step away, so close we could reach it with one bound. We circled it. It didn't move. We rested. When the rays of the sun lit up its jagged ridges, which looked like a dead man's spine, the whole group stopped. We all looked for a rock to put our heads under, to keep them in the shade and sleep a few hours. Our legs and feet we left in the sun, to warm and dry them. It was so hot it tore our skin off, but what the hell?

At sunset they made us get up and we set off again. It was the fifth night.

Agha, please, how long is it before we get to the top of the mountain?

A couple of hours, he replied without looking at me.

I joined the group.

What did he say?

Nothing. Shut up and walk.

We Afghans were the youngest, the most used to stones and heights, the blazing sun, the freezing snow. But this mountain was endless, a maze. The peak was always there, but we never seemed to reach it. Ten days and ten nights dripped away, one after the other, like water dripping from a stalactite.

Early one morning—it was dark and we were clambering over the rocks on our hands and knees—a Bengali boy got into difficulty. I don't know what it was, maybe a breathing problem, or maybe his heart, but he fell and slid down over the snow for several meters. We started yelling, Wait, someone's dying here, we have to stop and help him, but the traffickers (there were five of them) fired in the air with their Kalashnikovs.

Anyone who doesn't start walking again immediately stays here forever, they said.

We tried to help the young Bengali, to take him by the arms and under the armpits, to help him up and get him to walk, but it was too much for us. He was too heavy, we were too tired, too everything. It wasn't possible. We abandoned him. As we rounded a bend, I could still hear his voice for a moment. Then it faded completely, swallowed by the wind.

On the fifteenth day there was a knife fight between a Kurd and a Pakistani. I don't know what they were fighting over, food maybe, or maybe nothing at all. The Kurd ended up the loser. We abandoned him, too.

On the sixteenth day, for the first time, I talked to a Pakistani boy who wasn't much older than I was (Afghans and Pakistanis didn't usually talk much to each other). As we walked—we were in one of those areas where the wind wasn't too bad and we were able to speak—I asked him where he was heading, what he planned to do and where he planned to go after we got to Istanbul. He didn't reply immediately. He seemed lost in thought. He looked at me as if he wasn't sure he'd understood the question, with the kind of expression on his face that seemed to say, *What an idiot!* London, he said, walking faster to get away from me. Later, I discovered that all the Pakistanis were the same. They never said Turkey or Europe. They just said London. If any of them was in a good mood and asked me, How about you? I would say, Somewhere.

On the eighteenth day I saw a group of people sitting

on the ground. I saw them in the distance and couldn't figure out at first why they'd stopped. The wind was like a razor and my nose was clogged with snow, but when I tried to wipe it away with my fingers, it was no longer there. All at once, we turned a sharp bend and there they were, that group of people sitting on the ground. They'd be sitting there forever. They were frozen. They were dead. I have no idea how long they'd been there. All the others sidled silently past them. I stole the shoes from one of them, because mine were ruined and my toes had turned purple. I couldn't feel them anymore, even if I hit them with a stone. I took the shoes and tried them on. They fitted me well. They were much better than mine. I raised my hand in a gesture of gratitude. I think about him every now and then.

Every day, twice a day, they gave us an egg, a tomato and a piece of bread. New supplies arrived on a horse. But now we were too high for that. On the twenty-second day they handed out the last rations. They told us to divide them into pieces to make them last, but an egg, a boiled egg, is a hard thing to divide.

The others summoned up the courage to push me forward. Ask, they said.

What's the point? I replied.

Never mind, just ask.

Are we nearly there? I asked one of the traffickers.

Yes, he said, we're nearly there. But I didn't believe him.

And yet, on the twenty-sixth day, the mountain came to an end. One step, another, then another, and all of a sudden we stopped climbing. There was nothing more to climb, we'd reached the top. This was where the Iranians handed us over to the Turks. At that point, for the first time since the beginning of our trek, we did another head count. Twelve people were missing. Twelve, out of the group of seventy-seven, had died during the walk. Mostly Bengalis and Pakistanis. Vanished into the silence, and I hadn't even noticed. We looked at each other as if we'd never seen each other before, as if it hadn't been us walking. Our faces were red and in ruins. The lines were cuts, the cracks bled.

The Turks who were waiting for us there made us sit down on the ground in concentric circles, to protect ourselves from the cold. Every half hour we had to change places. Those in the middle had to move to the outside so that everyone could take turns getting warm and feeling the cold wind of the world on their backs.

On the twenty-seventh day—I know it was the twenty-seventh because I carry each and every one of those days around my neck like the beads of a necklace— we came down off the mountain and the mountain slowly turned into hills and woods and meadows and streams and fields and all the wonderful things there are on earth. In the spots where there weren't any trees, they made us run in groups, keeping our heads down. Sometimes they open fire, they said.

Who?

It doesn't matter who. Sometimes they open fire.

After two days—two more days, two days that could have been two years or two centuries—we reached Van.

Van is also on a lake. Lake Van. Our journey had been a journey from one lake to another. On the outskirts of this Turkish town, the first Turkish town we stopped in, we sneaked into a field and spent the night sleeping in the tall grass. Some Turkish peasants, friends of the traffickers, were nice to us and brought us something to eat and drink. I would have liked to change my clothes, the ones I was wearing were dirty and torn, like rags to clean the floor with, but the nice clothes I'd bought in Teheran I had to keep for Istanbul, I couldn't run the risk of getting them dirty and smelly before time, I really couldn't.

Before dawn they had us jumping out of the grass like crickets, loaded us in a lorry and drove us to another place nearby. It was a kind of huge cowshed with a very high ceiling, a cowshed for illegals instead of cows, and they made the Afghans sleep next to the Pakistanis, which is never a good idea. That night there was a quarrel over space and a fight broke out. The Turks were forced to intervene and separate us. They didn't discriminate: they hit everyone.

We were stuck in that cowshed for four days.

One night, while we were sleeping, the roar of an engine started the walls shaking. The Turks told us to gather our things together and hurry. They rounded us up against the wall by ethnic group and started letting us out a few at a time, I assume to stop those inside from seeing what was happening outside and where they were putting us. We stood in a corner for about ten minutes, clutching our rucksacks to our chests, then someone called us and we went out.

The first thing was, the vehicle with the noisy engine had its lights on, and they were aimed straight at the door, so I was blinded. The second thing was, the vehicle with the noisy engine turned out to be a lorry, a huge lorry with a huge trailer which seemed to be full of stones and gravel.

Come around this end, they said.

We walked around to the back of the trailer.

Get in, they said.

Where? All we could see was the gravel and the stones, and dust in the beams of light.

The trafficker pointed downward. I thought he meant we should get underneath the lorry, but then I took a closer look—which should have made me believe what I was seeing, but I didn't want to believe it—and I realized that between the bed of the trailer, which carried the gravel and the stones, and the underside of the lorry—where the axle shaft was, to make things clearer—there was a small space, maybe fifty centimeters high, or slightly more. In other words, the lorry had a false bottom. A fifty-centimeter-high space in which to sit with our arms clasped around our legs and our knees against our chests and our necks bent to keep our heads wedged between our knees.

They gave each of us two bottles: one full and one empty. The full one was full of water. The empty one was to pee into.

They filled the false bottom with us, all of us, the fifty or however many of us there were. We weren't just cramped, we were very cramped. More than cramped. We were like grains of rice squeezed in someone's hand. When they closed the hatch, the darkness obliterated us. I felt suffocated. Let's hope it's a short journey, I thought. Let's hope it doesn't last long. A voice was moaning somewhere. I could feel the weight of the stones on the back of my neck, the weight of the air and the night on the stones, the weight of the sky and the stars. I started breathing through my nose, but I was breathing dust. I started breathing with my mouth, but my chest hurt. I would have liked to breathe with my ears or my hair, like plants, which gather humidity in the air, from the air. But I wasn't a plant, and there was no oxygen. We're stopping, I thought at one point. But it was only a traffic junction. On another occasion I thought, We're there now, we're there. But it was the driver who'd got out to have a pee. I heard him. (Nothing escapes me, oh, no.) By the time I next said to myself, We've arrived, my knees and shoulders were dead. But it was a false alarm: I don't know why we'd stopped that time.

After a while, I stopped existing. I stopped counting the seconds or imagining our arrival. My thoughts and my muscles were weeping. My fatigue and my bones were weeping. Smells. I remember the smells. Pee and sweat. Screams, from time to time, and voices in the dark. I don't know how much time had passed when I heard someone moaning horribly, as if they were having their nails pulled out. I thought it was a dream at first, I thought the hoarse voice mixed with the noise of the engine wasn't real. Water, he was saying. That one word: *water*. But he was saying it in a way I can't describe. I knew who it was, I'd recognized him. I also started to cry out, Water, just to do something, to say, Help, there's someone dying, but nobody responded. Drink your own pee, I said, because he wouldn't stop crying, but I don't know if he heard. He didn't reply, just kept on moaning. It was unbearable. So I started crawling on my belly through the mass of bodies, with people punching and pinching me as I passed, which is understandable, because I was squashing them. I reached the boy. I couldn't see him, but with my hands I groped for his face, his nose, his mouth. He was moaning, repeating, Water, water, water. I asked someone nearby if they still had any left in their bottle, because mine was finished, but everyone had drunk every drop. I slid over the bodies again until I found a Bengali boy who said, Yes, he still had some water at the bottom of his bottle, but no, he wouldn't give it to me. I said, I beg you. He said no. I implored him, Just a sip. He said no, and as he was saying no I was trying to figure out where his no was coming from. I threw a punch at the no. I felt his teeth against my fist and when he cried out I slapped him over and over, not to hurt him, just to find the bottle. As soon as I felt it, I grabbed hold of it in my hand and disappeared—which was the easiest thing in the world to do in that place. I took the boy the remaining water, which made me feel good, if only for a short time, it made me feel human.

It lasted three days. We never got out. The door was never opened.

Then a light.

An electric light.

———

I've been told that it's like waking up from a general anesthetic. The outlines of things are blurred, and you feel as if you're rolling down a hill, inside a wheel, the kind of thing that happened in Telisia and Sang Safid. They made us roll out onto the ground because nobody could move even the little finger of one hand. Our blood had stopped flowing, our feet were swollen, our necks stiff. They started with those closest to the hatch, letting them fall like sacks of onions. Then two Turks clambered right inside the space under the false bottom and grabbed those of us who hadn't yet moved. Every movement we made was extremely painful.

They pushed me into a corner and I stayed there, huddled up, for I don't know how long. I was a tangle of flesh.

Then my eyes gradually became accustomed to the light, and I saw where I was. It was an underground garage, filled with hundreds and hundreds of people. A kind of marshaling yard for immigrants, or something like that, a cave in the belly of Istanbul.

When I was finally able to move and breathe I looked for a place to pee, all the pee I hadn't been able to pass during the journey, all the pee I'd held in for three days. They showed me the (only) toilet, a hole in the floor. But when I tried to pee, a searing pain shook my legs and stomach, and I was afraid I was going to faint. I closed my eyes to summon up strength, I closed my eyes and when I opened them again I saw that my pee was red.

I was peeing blood. I peed blood for the next few weeks.

The others were standing in line to use a telephone. Each person had to call his trafficker in Iran, the one he'd made arrangements with before the journey, in my case Farid's cousin. We had to phone both the trafficker and the person who was looking after the money so that the trafficker could get paid.

Only when the Iranian trafficker had his money, and only then, would he call his Turkish accomplices, here in the garage in Istanbul, to say that everything was okay and they could free the prisoners: us.

Hello? Enaiatollah Akbari. I'm in Istanbul.

Three days later, they blindfolded me and made me get in a car together with some other Afghan boys. They drove us around the city for a while so that we wouldn't know where we'd come from, which hole had spewed us out, and then they left us in a park. But not all together. One here and one there.

I waited until the car had left before taking off my blindfold. Around me were the lights of the city. Around me was the city. I realized—and I only really became aware of it at that moment—that I'd made it. I sat down on a low wall and stayed there for a few hours, motionless, staring straight ahead of me, in that place I didn't know. There was a smell of fried food and flowers. And the sea. And maybe I'd changed, or maybe it was Istanbul that was different, or Turkey, I don't know, but the fact is that, having always liked to have a roof over my head at night, from the *samavat* Qgazi onward, now that I was here I didn't even look for a place to stay but was content to spend my nights in the park, and I did that for quite a while.

I tried to make contact with the Afghan community, but without much success. But I did discover that there was a place near a bazaar in a rundown area over toward the Bosphorus where you could go early in the morning in the hope of finding work. You sat and waited until someone arrived in a car and got out and said, I can offer you such and such for such and such money. If you said yes, you got up and went with him. You worked all day, you worked hard, and in the evening you were paid what had been arranged.

It was much harder trying to live a decent life in Istanbul than in Iran. And sometimes I wondered, What have I done? Then I remembered the repatriations to Herat and everything, the roadblocks, the shaved hair, and it struck me that, when you got down to it, I was fine in that park in Istanbul. There were people, other migrants, who let me take a shower in their house. I could pick up a bit of food here and there. The days flowed over me and life around me, like a river. I was turning into a rock.

Then one evening, after a game of football in the back alleys, some Afghan boys who were younger than me told me they would soon be leaving for Greece. A man had put them in touch with a clothing factory, where they were going to work for nothing, and after a few months this man would help them get to Greece.

How?

In a dinghy.

Another journey? I thought of the mountains. I thought of the fake bottom in the lorry. I thought, Now the sea. It scared me. I could barely stay afloat in a river. In the open sea, the Mediterranean, I would drown. I had no idea what was in the sea.

I want to find work in Istanbul, I said.

You won't find any.

I want to try.

There's no work for us here in Turkey. We have to go west.

I want to find work in Istanbul, I repeated. And for another couple of months that was what I tried to do. I tried as hard as I could, but it wasn't easy, it really wasn't.

And when something's so hard that it becomes impossible, all you can do is stop trying and think of an alternative. Don't you agree?

By the time the fateful day was approaching when those Afghan boys were supposed to leave for Greece, I was beginning to think that I might have done better to accept their invitation. But it was too late now. They'd worked to pay for the journey.

So I made up a lie. If you want to go to Greece, I said, it's better if I come with you, because it's likely you'll need someone with you who can speak English, and I speak English. If you pay for me, too, I said, and I come with you, you'll be able to communicate with the Greeks, ask them for help or information or whatever. What do you say? I'd be useful to you. I hoped they'd fall for it, because they were all a bit younger than me, and much less wise about the ways of the world.

Really? they said.

Really what?

Do you really speak English?

Yes.

Let's hear.

What do you want to hear?

Say something in English.

So I said one of the few words I knew: *house.*

What does that mean?

I told them.

And they accepted.

Where did you learn English?

From people I met. When you get it into your head that you're going to emigrate it's good to know a bit of English. Lots of people were trying to get to London, and sometimes I helped friends to rehearse a few useful phrases.

So you really could speak it.

No, I couldn't. I knew a few words. Like ship, *and* port, *things like that.*

Did they ever find out?

Wait and see.

That week, while waiting to leave, I worked for three days—I was lucky—and earned enough to buy new clothes to wear in Greece. You always need new clothes when you arrive in a place where you're a nobody.

There were five of us: Rahmat, Liaqat, Hussein Ali, Soltan and me.

Hussein Ali was the youngest, he was twelve.

From Istanbul we went to Ayvalik, which was on the Turkish coast opposite the Greek island of Lesbos. We were taken from Istanbul to Ayvalik by the trafficker, a mustached Turk with pockmarked skin, who had said—I don't remember the exact words, but this was the gist of it—that he would tell us how to get to Greece.

And he did. When we got to Ayvalik, he switched off the engine of the van, took from the bonnet a cardboard box gnawed by mice, dragged us up a hill at sunset, pointed at the sea and said, Greece is that way, good luck.

As I've said, whenever anyone wishes me good luck, things go wrong. And anyway, what did it mean, Greece is that way? All I could see was sea.

But he was just as scared as us, because what he was doing was illegal, so he abandoned us at the top of the hill and left, mumbling something in Turkish.

We opened the cardboard box. It contained the dinghy (the deflated dinghy, of course), the oars (there were even two spare ones), the pump, the adhesive tape—at the time I thought: adhesive tape?—and the life jackets. It was like an IKEA flatpack for illegals. With instructions and everything. We divided the things among us, put on the life jackets, because it was easier to wear them than to carry them, and walked down toward the woods that divided the hill from the beach. We were something like three or four kilometers from the beach, and in the meantime darkness had fallen. In those years, now that I think of it, I lived more in the dark than the light.

So anyway, we started walking toward the beach and

there was this big wood with darkness filling the spaces between the trees and not even twenty minutes had gone by when we heard noises, strange noises, not the wind in the branches and the leaves. No, something else.

Must be cows, Rahmat said.

Must be goats, Hussein Ali said.

Goats don't make a noise like that, stupid.

Hussein Ali punched Rahmat in the shoulder. Neither do cows for that matter, idiot.

They started pushing each other and fighting.

Be quiet, I said. Stop it.

They must be wild cows, said Liaqat. A kind of wild cow you only find in Turkey. But we didn't have time to comment on this statement by Liaqat, because just then these cows of his suddenly appeared on the path, running toward us. They ran like devils, these wild cows, and they were short, short and squat. Run, cried Hussein Ali, the wild cows are coming. And we started running hell for leather until we found a ditch, or something like that, and dived in and hid among the shrubs.

We waited for silence to fall again and after a while Liaqat put his head out and said, Hey, they aren't cows. They're pigs.

Wild pigs, Hussein Ali said.

Wild pigs, Liaqat repeated.

They were boars. But none of us had ever seen a boar.

We waited until they'd gone away, then climbed out of the ditch and set off again along the path to the beach.

Ten minutes later, we heard barking.

Those are dogs, said Hussein Ali.

Congratulations, said Liaqat. I can see you're educated. Can you also recognize the noise a sheep makes? And a horse?

They started pushing each other and quarreling, but immediately stopped because, just then, a dog appeared from behind a tree. First one, then another. Then a third one. Then the barking of the dogs got closer and we saw them on our right, standing on a rock. They weren't behind a gate or anything, they were free. And there were lots of them.

Wild dogs, cried Hussein Ali. This country is full of wild things.

The dogs jumped down from the rock, with steam coming out of their mouths and their tails up in the air, and we started running again, as fast as an avalanche, and once again we dived into a ditch, which this time was much deeper than we had thought, and we rolled down until we ended up on the bank of a dried-up stream.

The dinghy, I cried. Don't make a hole in the dinghy.

We moved all the stones and debris out of the way, and when we finally managed to get up, none of us were seriously hurt. Scratches and bruises, yes, but nothing permanent. And we still had the dinghy and the pump and everything. That was when I noticed Liaqat's life jacket.

Liaqat, I said, your jacket is torn.

Liaqat took it off and turned it over and over, but there was nothing to be done. It was unusable. He looked at me in desperation, then gave a twisted smile. So's yours, he said. He approached Hussein Ali. So's Hussein Ali's.

Not a single jacket was still intact.

But we're on the beach, said Rahmat.

Yes, we're on the beach, echoed Hussein Ali.

Is there a school where they teach you to state the obvious? said Liaqat.

Quick, let's inflate the dinghy, suggested Rahmat.

It's too late.

What?

It's too late, I repeated. We have to wait till tomorrow.

It isn't true, we can make it.

The trafficker had told us it took about three hours to cross the strip of sea separating us from Lesbos. But it must have been about two or three in the morning by now and the risk was that we would arrive in the first light of dawn, when we might well be seen. We needed darkness and invisibility. We needed to do things properly. We had to wait for the following night.

I'm the oldest, I said. I'm the captain. Let's put it to the vote. Who's in favor of leaving tomorrow night?

Hussein Ali was the first to raise his hand, followed immediately by Soltan and Rahmat.

Liaqat sighed. Then let's get some rest, he said. Not too close to the sea, if possible. He threw a pointed glance at Hussein Ali. We don't want a wild wave to attack us while we sleep, do we?

Hussein Ali didn't get the joke. He nodded and said, Or a crocodile. And he said it seriously, with his eyes wide open.

There aren't any crocodiles in the sea, Liaqat said.

How do you know?

I just know, stupid.

Well, you're talking rubbish. You can't even swim.

You can't swim either.

That's true. Hussein Ali shrugged. That's why I'm afraid of crocodiles.

But there aren't any. Can't you get that into your head? There. Aren't. Any. They live in rivers.

I wouldn't be so sure of that, whispered Hussein Ali, looking at the water and shifting a small stone with the tip of his foot. There could be all kinds of things down there in that darkness.

———

It was a good day, the next day, a really good day, even though we'd used up all our supplies of food and water. Soltan tried to drink water from the sea, and after the first mouthful he started to scream that the water was poisoned, that the Turks and Greeks had poisoned it to kill us. We kept ourselves to ourselves (well there wasn't anyone else), slept for a long time and built traps for wild pigs. We didn't think about the dangers of the crossing. Death is always a distant thought, even when you feel it close. You think you'll make it, and so will your friends.

Around midnight we came out into the open. We moved the equipment close to the rocks, to be protected and not be seen by passing boats. The dinghy had to be inflated with the pump, a pump with a balloon that you pressed with your foot. It was a blue and yellow dinghy—not all that big, to tell the truth, and the maximum weight it was intended for was lower than the combined weight of the five of us, but we pretended not to notice.

We were so busy inflating the dinghy and setting up the oars that we didn't see a light approaching, a light at sea.

It was Rahmat who saw it. Look, he said.

We turned our heads in unison.

Out on the water, I couldn't say how far out, a boat was passing, with red and green lights flashing at the sides, and it may have been those red and green lights or something else, but we became convinced it was the coast guard. It's the coast guard, we said. Did they see us? we asked each other in panic. Could they have seen us? Who knows? How can we know? We deflated the dinghy, ran back up the beach and dived back into the undergrowth.

It was a fishing boat, almost certainly.

What should we do?

Best to wait.

For how long?

An hour.

What if they come back?

Tomorrow, then.

Best to wait until tomorrow.

Yes, yes. Tomorrow.

Shall we sleep?

Let's sleep.

What about guard duty?

What guard duty?

We ought to take turns at guard duty, said Hussein Ali.

We don't need guard duty.

If they saw us, they'll come looking for us.

But maybe they didn't see us.

Then we can leave.

No, we can't leave, Hussein Ali. And besides, if they

came looking for us, we'd notice. You can't park a boat on a beach without making a noise. If you want to, you can take first turn at guard duty.

Why me?

Because you suggested it, that's why.

Who should I wake up after me?

Wake me, I said.

All right.

Good night.

Good night.

When Hussein Ali started talking in his sleep I was still awake. Anyway, there wasn't really a need to keep guard.

On the third evening, we had a discussion and decided to leave a bit earlier. Since the boat had passed at midnight, then it was just possible, we calculated, that at ten they would still be having dinner or watching television. So a couple of hours after sunset we went to the rocks, inflated the dinghy and put it in the water. We stripped down to our pants.

As I've already said, I was the oldest, and I was also the only one who could swim a little. The others not only couldn't swim, they were more scared than I can say. When the time came to get into the water to hold the dinghy still and let everyone get in, I stepped forward, like a hero, and put a foot down where I thought I'd find the seabed, though I had no idea what the seabed was like. That was how I discovered that even in the sea there's rock. Boys, I said, there's rock in the sea. And they all said, Really? I was just about to reply Yes when, attempting another step, I slipped and ended up with my whole body in the water. Groping with my hands, my arms stiff, I managed not to drown. I grabbed hold of the dinghy and held it steady so that the others could get in.

Hurry up, said Hussein Ali. The crocodiles will eat your feet.

Liaqat gave him a slap on the head.

If not a crocodile, he said, maybe a whale.

With the help of Soltan and Rahmat I climbed on board.

Then what did we do? We grabbed hold of the oars and started hitting the surface of the water really hard, as if trying to give it a thrashing, so hard that I even broke an oar. Our strokes were fairly random, because if one thing was certain it was that none of us could row. We all rowed on one side. When we rowed on the right, the dinghy veered to the right, and when we rowed on the left, the dinghy veered to the left.

What with one thing and another, we ended up on the rocks.

Now I don't know how dinghies are made, but ours must have had two layers of inflatable rubber, because although it got a hole in it, it didn't sink.

Still, we needed to fix it.

With a huge effort, we managed to get back to land and pull the dinghy up onto the shingle.

Fortunately we had the adhesive tape (so that was what it was for), and we patched up the hole with it. But we weren't sure that it would hold so we decided that Hussein Ali, who was the smallest of us, would keep his hands pressed on the patch instead of rowing.

Rahmat and I took up position on the left.

Liaqat and Soltan on the right.

Now, I said. And the four of us started to paddle.

At last, we set off.

Greece

The sea started to get rough about midnight, I think, or thereabout. We were rowing fast, but we couldn't shout out encouragement to each other, the way professionals do, who always have someone either behind them or in front saying, *And one and two, and one and two*, and so on, because rowers row in unison. We couldn't, because we didn't want to make a noise, we were afraid even to sneeze—which, as we were half naked, wearing nothing but underpants (we'd packed our clothes into plastic bags which we'd sealed with adhesive tape to stop water getting in)—was something that might well happen. We were afraid to sneeze because we thought the coast guard would pick up our sneezing on their radar over the noise of the waves.

We'd been told that by rowing fast we would land on the coast of Greece in two or three hours, but that was without taking into account the water coming into the dinghy. When the sea got rough and started pouring down on us as if it was raining, I took a water bottle, tore it in half with my teeth to make it into a bowl and said to Hussein Ali, Leave the patch and start throwing the water back in the sea.

How?

With this, I said, showing him the half bottle. At that moment a wave ripped it out of my hand, as if it had heard me and didn't agree. I made another one. I took Hussein Ali's hand and pressed the bowl into it. With this, I said again.

We were still rowing. But why then did we feel as if we weren't moving? Or worse still, that we were going backward? And as if that wasn't enough, the inflatable tubes got in the way, the inflatable tubes we'd been given to use as life preservers. We'd tied them to the dinghy with long ropes because we were afraid they'd bother us as we rowed, so unfortunately, when the wind blew hard, it lifted these inflatable tubes, turning them into balloons that made the dinghy rotate or swerve.

Every now and again, the current or the wind or the waves threw us back toward the coast of Turkey—or so we assumed, because when we were tossed about like that, we weren't really sure which way was Turkey and which way was Greece—and little Hussein Ali, still collecting the water that was filling the dinghy, started whining. I know why we can't get to Greece, he said. We can't get to Greece because the sea goes uphill in that direction.

Our point of reference was a lighthouse on the Greek coast. But after a while we stopped seeing it. The waves were so high they covered it, and at that point Hussein Ali started screaming, We're only as big as a whale's tooth. And the whales will eat us. And if they don't eat us the crocodiles will, even though you say there aren't any. We have to turn back, we have to turn back.

I'm not turning back, I said. We're near Greece, and if we aren't near, at least we're halfway by now. It's the same distance, so it makes no difference if we go on or turn back, and I prefer to die in the sea rather than start this whole journey all over again.

We started arguing, right there in the middle of the sea, with the darkness and the waves all around, and with Rahmat and me saying, To Greece, to Greece. And Soltan and Liaqat saying, To Turkey, to Turkey. And Hussein Ali still bailing water and crying and saying, The mountain's falling, the mountain's falling, because the waves were so high—two or three meters or even more—that when they towered over us, when the dinghy was in the hollow between one wave and the next, it was as if they were about to collapse on top of us. But instead they lifted us right up and, when we were on the crest, let us down again with a bump, like the carousels I've been on here in Italy, at the amusement park. But, right then, it wasn't amusing at all.

So the situation was this: Rahmat and me rowing like mad toward Greece (or in the direction we thought Greece was), while Soltan and Liaqat were rowing toward Turkey (or in the direction they thought Turkey was). The argument degenerated into name calling, and we started hitting and elbowing each other like complete idiots, in a dinghy that was just a little dot in the middle of nowhere, while Hussein Ali was crying and saying, What's going on? I'm doing my job of throwing out the water and you're hitting each other? Row. Please, just row.

I think it was then that the boat appeared. Or rather, not the boat, the ship. A very big ship, a ferry or something like that. I saw it coming up behind Hussein Ali as he spoke. It passed very, very close to us.

How close?

Do you see the florist's shop outside the window? The distance from here to there.

As close as that?

As close as from here to there.

These high waves were different from normal waves. They got mixed up with the others, and the dinghy made a strange movement, like a horse stung by a bee. And Liaqat couldn't hold on. I felt his fingers slide over my shoulder. He didn't scream, he didn't have time. The dinghy had suddenly tossed him out.

Let me get this right. Liaqat fell into the water?
Yes.
And what did the rest of you do?
We looked for him as best we could, hoping to see him in among the waves, and we shouted. But he'd disappeared.

When the waves from the ship—which didn't stop: maybe it saw us, maybe not, we couldn't tell—anyway, when the waves subsided, we kept rowing and calling Liaqat's name. And rowing. And calling. Turning in circles around the spot where we'd been, or so we thought, though in all probability we'd already moved a long way from there.

Nothing. Liaqat had been taken by the darkness.

At that point, I'm not really sure what happened: it may have been exhaustion, it may have been discouragement, it may have been that we felt too small, infinitely too small not to succumb to all of these things—but at that point we fell asleep.

———

By the time we opened our eyes again, it was dawn. The water around us was dark, almost black. We rinsed our faces, spitting out the salt. We looked along the horizon and saw land. A strip of land, with a beach and a hill. It wasn't too far away. We could make it. We started rowing quickly and painfully, without knowing whether it was Greece or Turkey. We simply said, Let's row in that direction.

After being on our knees for so long, our legs had gone numb. We had tiny little cuts on our hands: we didn't know how we'd got them, but they burned every time the salt water made them wet. As we approached the island, the sky grew lighter, and it was then that Soltan saw a flag on a hill. All he said, in a thin voice, was, A flag. He pointed with his index finger. It kept flapping in the wind, but at those moments when it was fully stretched we could see horizontal stripes, alternately blue and white (nine stripes in all), starting with a blue stripe at the top, and in the upper corner, on the same side as the pole, a square, also blue, with a white cross in the middle.

The flag of Greece.

Reaching shallow water, we got out of the dinghy. We dragged it ashore, close to the rocks, our backs stooped so as to be as inconspicuous as possible, although there didn't seem to be anybody about. We deflated the dinghy, first squeezing the air through the plugs, then, getting impatient, ripping the plastic with stones. We folded it quickly and hid it under a rock, and covered the rock with sand. We looked at each other.

What shall we do? asked Hussein Ali.

We were in our underpants. We'd lost our clothes. What could we do?

Stay here, I said.

Where are you going?

To the village.

What village? We don't know where we are.

On the coast . . .

On the coast, said Soltan. Congratulations.

Let me finish, I said. We were supposed to get to Mytilene, right?

Do you know which way Mytilene is?

No. But there has to be a village around here. A few houses. Some shops. I'll look for food and even some clothes, if possible. You wait here. There's no point wandering around like four stray dogs, getting ourselves noticed.

I want to come too, said Hussein Ali.

No.

Why?

I've already explained.

Because you can hide better when you're alone, said Rahmat.

Hussein Ali gave me a dirty look. Make sure you come back.

I'll be back as soon as I can.

You won't leave us, will you?

I turned away without replying and set off along the path that climbed the hill. I walked for a long time, without knowing where I was going. I may even have got lost, which is quite possible when you don't know where you're going.

The houses appeared out of nowhere, behind the trees. In among the houses was a supermarket. There were groups of tourists, families on holiday, elderly people out for a stroll. An ice-cream parlor with a long queue in front of it. A newsagent's. A garage that hired out scooters and cars. And a little square with benches and a playground. From the ice-cream parlor came cheerful music, played very loud.

The supermarket. The supermarket was paradise. The supermarket was my target. All I had to do was go in, take some food, nothing too difficult, fruit would do, and clothes, maybe bathing trunks, if they had any. Young boys walking around in bathing trunks in a seaside resort is one thing, but young boys walking around in their underpants, well, that's another matter entirely.

A police car passed. I hid behind (more inside than behind) a flowerbed. I squatted there for a few minutes watching the movements at the front of the supermarket, to see if I could get in without attracting attention, and came to the conclusion that there was no way I could go in through the front. But I could always go around the back. So I flattened myself against the walls of the houses like a lizard, slid under a gate, getting a couple of nasty scratches on the stomach in the process, and finally climbed a metal fence. I entered the supermarket like a ghost, taking advantage of the fact that the assistant unloading boxes of snacks was too busy to notice me. As I placed my bare foot on the cold, slippery tiles of the section of the supermarket selling household goods, I heard voices I recognized coming from behind a shelf. I poked my head around.

Rahmat, Hussein Ali and Soltan were strolling along the aisles, watched from a distance by a bewildered young blond assistant.

They'd disobeyed. I had no idea how they'd managed to get there before me. I stepped out, signaling to them to act normally and pretend we didn't know each other.

Each of us took something for himself: food but no clothes, because they didn't sell them. People were looking at us in astonishment, wide-eyed. We had to hurry. But, when we tried to leave, we found the door of the store-room at the back was blocked. There was still the main door, but to get out that way we'd have to make a run for it. As we sped down the fruit and vegetable aisle, then the toiletries aisle, then some other aisle I can't remember, I wondered if the person yelling in Greek was the manager, and if the manager who was hurling insults at us in Greek had picked up his Greek telephone to call the Greek police. Oh, if only those three idiots had waited for me! I would have done everything differently, much more discreetly. Instead of which, we hurtled out through the glass door—without crashing into anyone, thank God—but no sooner had we taken a few steps along the pavement, surrounded by children with ice cream running down over their fingers and little old ladies in silvery sandals and people with scared looks on their faces (although I doubt young boys in their underpants could really scare anyone), than a police car slammed on the brakes—just like in the films, I swear—and three huge policemen got out.

I hardly had time to even be aware of this police car before I was inside it. With Hussein Ali. In the backseat. Just the two of us.

The others had apparently managed to get away.

———

Pakistanis?

No.

Afghans?

No.

I know you're Afghans. Don't mess me around.

No Afghans, no.

Oh, no Afghans no? Afghans yes, you little rats. Afghans. I can recognize you from the smell.

They dragged us to the police station, and shut us up in a little room. We could hear steps in the corridor and voices saying things we didn't understand, and I remember that what I was afraid of more than anything else, more than being beaten or put in prison, was being fingerprinted. I had heard all about this fingerprinting business from some boys who worked at the stonecutting factory in Iran. They'd told me that in Greece, as soon as they caught you, they took your fingerprints, and if you were illegal you were screwed, because after that you couldn't ask for political asylum in any other country in Europe.

So Hussein Ali and I decided to make nuisances of ourselves in order to get thrown out before the fingerprint people arrived. But to get thrown out you have to be a serious nuisance, a professional. First of all, we started whining and yelling that we had stomachaches because we were hungry, and the policemen brought us dry biscuits. Then that we had to go to the toilet. We kept saying, Toilet, toilet. After the toilet we started crying and shouting and moaning, and kept it up until night fell. Police on night duty are usually less patient, and if things go badly they hit you till you bleed, but if things go well they let you go.

We took the risk. Things went well.

It was almost morning, still dark, and with very few cars around, when two of the policemen, fed up with our yelling, threw open the door of the little room and, dragging us by our ears, flung us into the street, shouting at us to go back where we'd come from, bunch of screaming monkeys. Or something like that.

We spent the whole morning searching for Soltan and Rahmat. We found them outside the town, near the beach, but I didn't have time to be pleased at finding them because I immediately lost my temper. I'd been hoping they'd have found some clothes in the meantime—trousers, T-shirts or whatever, maybe shoes—but they hadn't found a thing. All four of us still looked like tramps, and it isn't true that you can't judge a book by its cover, you can.

One thing I'd done while I was in the police station (as an illegal, you have to be able to exploit every opportunity) had been to have a good look at a large map of the island on the wall: the place where we were was marked in red, Mytilene in blue. It was from Mytilene that you could catch a boat for Athens. It might be a day's walk, through fields and along secondary roads, but we'd get there, even with aching feet.

We set off, walking along the edge of a road. The sun was hot enough to bake bread, even if you stood still you broke out in a sweat. Soltan was complaining—I don't think Hussein Ali had any breath left, otherwise he would have complained, too, as usual—and from time to time he would lean into the road and wave at the cars to stop and give us a lift, even though he was half naked. I dragged him away, saying, No. What are you doing? They'll call the police again. But he kept on doing it.

Let's stop here, I beg you, he said. Let's wait for someone to give us a ride.

If you carry on like that, I said, it'll be the police who pick you up. You'll see.

Not that I wanted to be the bird of ill omen, or whatever you call it. Not at all. It was in my own interest to continue the journey with them, so we could look out for each other, but they kept on and on about how tired they were and how much better it would be to get a lift from a small van or something like that, so finally I said, No, and walked away from the group.

Nearby there was a small shop with a petrol pump and to the right of it, a dirty, flaking old phone box half hidden by the branches of a tree. I went in, grabbed the telephone and pretended to be making a call, instead of which I was keeping my eyes on my companions, to see what they were up to.

When the police car arrived—with its lights on, but without a siren—I thought for a moment I should dash out and yell, Run away, run away, but I was too late. I huddled in the phone box and watched as they fled and the police caught up with them and beat them with truncheons. I saw it all from a kneeling position, through the dirty windows, unable to do anything, and praying that no one thought of making a phone call.

As soon as the police car had gone, with a screech of tires, I left the phone box, crept past the service station, making sure there was nobody around, and set off hell for leather along a sandy, deserted country lane. I kept on running, running, running, without knowing where I was going, until my lungs were ready to burst and I had to lie down on the ground to recover. When I realized I was fine, I got up and started walking again. After half an hour, I passed a courtyard. It was the courtyard of a private house, surrounded by a low wall and with a big tree in the middle. I didn't see anyone, so I climbed over.

There was a dog, but it was tied up. It saw me and started barking, and I hid under the thick branch of the tree.

I must have been tired. Because I fell asleep.

I can imagine you were pretty tired, Enaiat.
It wasn't only the fact that I was tired. There was something about that place that made me feel calm, you know?
What exactly?
I couldn't say. Some things you just feel.

After a while, the old lady who lived there came out. She woke me up, but gently. I leapt to my feet, and was going to run away, but she made me a sign to come inside. She gave me some good food to eat, vegetables and something else. She made me take a shower. She gave me some nice clothes, too: a shirt with blue stripes, jeans and a pair of white trainers. It was incredible that she had all those clothes in her house, and in my size. I don't know whose they were, maybe a grandson of hers.

The lady kept talking all the time, in Greek and English, and I didn't understand much. Whenever I saw her smile, I'd say, Good, good. Whenever she made a serious face, I'd also make a serious face, and shake my head from side to side: No, no.

In the afternoon, after I'd had my shower and got

dressed, the old lady went with me to the bus station, bought me a ticket (yes, she actually bought it for me), put fifty euros in my hand, a whole fifty euros, said good-bye and left. Yes, I thought, there really are some very strange and very kind people in the world.

There you go again.

What do you mean?

You tell me things, Enaiat, and then immediately you go on to something else. Tell me more about this lady. Describe her house.

Why?

What do you mean, why? I'm interested. Other people might be, too.

Yes, but I already told you. I'm only interested in what happened. The lady is important for what she did. Her name doesn't matter. What her house was like doesn't matter. She could have been anybody.

How do you mean, anybody?

Anybody could have behaved like that.

So, incredibly, I arrived in Mytilene. It's a big, busy city, Mytilene, with lots of tourists and shops and cars. I asked the way to the "ship station," using what I thought were the English words for the port where the ferries left for Athens. The people I asked answered in words, as people usually do, but I looked at the movements of their hands.

This way. That way.

When I got to the port, I came across a whole lot of other Afghan boys who'd been there for days and days wandering around and trying to buy a ticket, and every time they'd tried they'd been chased away, because it was obvious they weren't normal passengers, but illegals. That depressed me a bit. How long would I have to wait?

But that didn't happen to me.

Maybe it was because of how I was dressed, because I was clean, because my belly was full and I had that contented look you have on your face when you've eaten well. Whatever it was, when I got to the counter and asked for a ticket, the girl behind the counter replied, Thirty-eight euros. I couldn't believe it at first, so I said, Repeat? And she said again, Thirty-eight euros.

Through the opening, I passed her the fifty-euro note I'd got from the old Greek lady. The girl—who was quite pretty, incidentally, with big eyes and nice make-up— took it and gave me twelve euros change. Incredulously, I thanked her and went out.

You can imagine the other boys' faces when they saw me with the ticket in my hand. They all gathered around.

They wanted to know how I'd managed it and some wouldn't even believe I'd bought it myself. They said I'd got a real tourist to buy it for me. But I hadn't.

How did you do it? they asked.

I just asked, I replied. At the counter.

The ferry was huge. There were five decks. I went up to the top deck to get a better view of the horizon and was savoring with every part of my body the fact that I was sitting comfortably and relaxed in a chair, not kneeling in a dinghy or with my legs crossed in the false bottom of a lorry, when suddenly my nose started to bleed: it was the first time in my life I'd had a nosebleed.

I ran to the toilet to rinse my face. I stuck my head under the tap, and there I was, with my head bent over the washbasin and the blood flowing and—I don't really know how to explain it, but I felt as if it wasn't only the blood that was flowing out of me, it was everything I'd been through, the sand of the desert, the dust of the streets and the snow of the mountains, the salt of the sea and the lime of Isfahan, the stones of Qom and the sewage from the gutters of Quetta. By the time the blood stopped flowing, I felt great. Better than I'd ever felt in my life. I wiped my face.

As I was looking for somewhere else to sit, again on the top deck, and again so that I could look at the hori-

zon, I walked past a line of benches which were all occu-
pied, and to avoid a little girl who was playing I brushed
against someone's knee. I'm sorry, I said. I gave the boy
a fleeting glance and was about to walk away, but then
I stopped and gave him a closer look. It isn't possible, I
thought.

Jamal.

He looked up. Enaiatollah.

I'd met Jamal in Iran, in Qom, playing football in
the tournament between the factories. We hugged.

I didn't see you before, he said. I didn't see you in the
port.

I just arrived.

But I didn't even see you around Mytilene.

I only arrived on the island yesterday.

Impossible.

I swear.

How?

In a dinghy. From Ayvalik.

Impossible.

I swear.

Yesterday you were in a dinghy and today you're
already on a ferry?

It must be luck. In fact, I'm sure it's luck.

We sat down next to each other and chatted for the
rest of the journey. He'd spent four days in Mytilene

without managing to get a ticket for Athens, and in the end he'd given eighty euros to someone who spoke very good English to buy it for him. But the worst thing was that, at one point, the police had picked him up. And fingerprinted him.

We reached Athens about nine the next morning. Some of the passengers hurried down into the belly of the boat to get their cars, others embraced their relatives on the last step of the gangway, still others put their cases into the boots of taxis and joined the traffic. The port was full of people greeting each other and patting each other on the back. Jamal and I weren't expected by anybody, and didn't know which way to go. Not that it made us sad. It was just that it's strange seeing all those relaxed, calm, confident people around you when you're the only one to feel lost. But that's the way things are, isn't it?

Let's go and have breakfast, said Jamal. Let's get a coffee.

I had the twelve euros left over from the ticket, and he had some loose change. We went into a bar and bought two huge paper cups of very weak coffee, like filter coffee, to be drunk through straws. I tasted it. It was disgusting. I'm not drinking that, I said.

Don't drink it if you don't want to, said Jamal. But hold it in your hand.

In my hand?

Like a tourist. Let's walk carrying the coffee. That's what tourists do, isn't it?

It was afternoon by the time we ventured into the city. We got on the underground. Every four stops we got off and went to see where we were. Then we went back down and set off again in the same direction. After going in and out three times, we came out and saw a big park, and there were lots and lots of people there because there was a concert, right there in the park, which was called Dikastirion, if I remember correctly.

When you don't know what to do, it's not a bad idea to mingle with a crowd. And in the crowd we heard people speaking Afghan. Following the voices, we found ourselves in the middle of a small group of boys, more or less our age, some of them a bit older, playing football. Here's a piece of good advice: if you ever spend time as an illegal, look for the parks, you always find something good in a park.

When evening fell, we waited for those boys to go to their homes so that we could ask for hospitality and something to eat, because we'd made friends with them after the match. But after a while, when it got dark, we saw one of them slip under a tree and take out a cardboard box. Then another one did the same, and another. In other words, the park was their home. But we were hungry, as people usually are when they haven't eaten for several hours.

Isn't there an Afghan restaurant that can give us food? we asked.

Look, we're not in Kabul. We're in Greece. In Athens.

Thanks, anyway.

The park was their home. And it became our home. That first morning we woke up early, about five. Someone mentioned the name of a church where they gave you breakfast. We went there and I had some bread and yogurt. For lunch there was another church. But there, the priests had laid out a whole lot of Bibles in every language—even mine—in full view, next to the front entrance, and before eating you had to read a page of it or they wouldn't give you any food.

No way, I thought in a burst of pride. I'd rather die of starvation than be forced to read the Bible for food.

Except that, after a while, my stomach started rumbling loudly, louder than my pride. Damn that hunger. I wandered around for half an hour trying to hold out, until I felt as if my belly button was being prised open with a corkscrew. So I approached the church and stood in front of the Bible in my language, looking at a page and pretending to read for what seemed like a long enough time, making sure the attendants saw me. Then I went inside.

I ate bread and yogurt. Like breakfast that morning.

You were lucky last night, my neighbor said.

Jamal was trying to get another piece of bread from the priests or monks or whatever they were. I was licking the bottom of my yogurt pot.

Why? I asked.

Because nothing happened.

I stopped licking. What do you mean, nothing?

No police, for instance. Sometimes the police come and kick everyone out.

Do they arrest people?

No. They just kick us out and make us move on.

Where to?

Wherever we like. It's just to make life even harder for us. I think that's why they do it.

Ah.

But it's not just the police, the boy added.

Who else?

Older boys. Men. Who go with little boys.

Where do they go?

Men who like little boys.

Really?

Really.

That evening, Jamal and I looked for the darkest, most hidden corner of the park in order to be safe, although if you're forced to sleep in a park, you can't expect much in the way of safety.

The most incredible thing I got involved in during that summer in Athens was (in Greek) the Αγωνες της XXVIII Ολυμπιαδας, in other words, the Games (listen to this) of the Twenty-Eighth Olympiad: *Athens 2004.* To be specific, the big stroke of luck for me and all the illegals who were in Athens at the time was that a lot of running tracks and swimming pools and stadiums and sports complexes and other things were still unfinished, and the games were going to start soon. So, in order for the city not to lose face, there was a big need for undeclared laborers, and even the police turned a blind eye, I think.

Every now and again, migrants are a secret weapon.

I didn't even know what the Olympics were. I didn't find out until I went with other Afghan boys to a little square where they'd said we could find work and a car picked me up and took me to the stadium. There I discovered that, if I wanted, there was work for two months, every day, including Saturdays and Sundays. The work was actually well organized. Each task was given out on the basis of age. All I had to do, for example, was hold the little trees in the avenue while others dug holes to plant them in. In the evening you were paid in cash: forty-five euros. An excellent wage, for me at least.

I remember that one night, in the park, a man came and sat down next to Jamal and started slowly stroking him. A Greek guy with a beard and a flashy shirt. Jamal gave me a little kick to wake me up (the two of us slept side by side, to protect each other). Listen, Ena, he said, there's someone here who's stroking me.

Why? I said.

How should I know? He's stroking me, but I don't know why.

Is he bothering you?

No, he's just stroking me. He's stroking my hair.

Then I remembered what that guy had said in the soup kitchen at the Orthodox church. We jumped up and ran to some older boys. The man with the beard followed us, but when he saw the older boys surround us, and us pointing at him, he shrugged his shoulders and went away.

Once the Olympics started, there wasn't any more work, and we spent the mornings and afternoons walking around, without knowing where to go or what to do. That was when I started talking about leaving again.

London, they all said. You have to go to London. Or Norway, if you can. Or why not Italy? If you went to Italy you had to go to Rome and, once you were in Rome, you had to go to Ostiense, which apparently was a station. There was a park there with a pyramid where you could find Afghans. For me, the important thing about Italy was that a boy I knew, someone from my village, from Nava, had managed to get there. His name was Payam. I knew he was in Italy because someone had brought the news to our village. I didn't know which city he was in and I didn't have a phone number or anything, but if he was in Italy, maybe I could track him down. It would be difficult, but you never knew.

I'm leaving, I said to Jamal one day. We were with two other friends, having an ice cream. I have some money saved from the work I did for the Olympics, I said. I can buy a ticket and go as far as Corinth, or Patras, and there try to sneak onto a lorry.

I know a trafficker who might be able to help you, said one of the boys.

Really?

Of course, he said. But first, listen, you should still try asking the Greek authorities for political asylum for health reasons.

What do you mean, political asylum for health reasons?

Didn't you know? There's a place, a clinic, where

they take care of you if you're ill, and do tests on you if you think you are. And if they find out there's something wrong with you, they give you asylum because of your illness.

Is there really a place like that? Why didn't you tell me before?

Well, for instance, because they have to give you injections. Not everyone likes taking tests and being given injections. But if you've already made up your mind to leave, what difference does it make, right?

Do you know anyone who got a residence permit that way? Personally, I mean?

Yes, a Bengali boy. He was lucky. You may be, too.

All right.

All right what?

I'll go, I said. Tell me where it is.

It was an old building with colored windows, nothing like the other clinics I'd seen. You had to buzz the third floor on the entryphone. Jamal and the others would wait for me outside, because it would take a couple of hours. I buzzed. They opened without a word, and I went upstairs.

The entrance certainly looked like the waiting room of a clinic. There wasn't a counter or a nurse to ask for information, but there were four or five men sitting on chairs, two of them reading magazines, the others staring into space. I sat down, too, and waited my turn.

Suddenly a door opened, as if there'd been a gust of wind (there were four white doors) and a woman came out. She was naked. Stark naked. I opened my eyes wide, then lowered them, I would have liked to put those eyes of mine in my pocket, and put out the fire in my cheeks, but her appearance had caught me so off guard that any position I assumed, any move I made, any breath I took would have seemed awkward and out of place. I was petrified. The naked girl passed quite close to me, and I think she gave me a sidelong glance and smiled. Then she went through another door and disappeared. A man stood up and followed her. But then another woman appeared, and she was naked, too. All at once there were something like a dozen of them, coming in and out. In the end—

In the end, Enaiat?

I stood up and ran out. I ran down the stairs, six steps at a time, and opened the front door, still running, and almost got myself knocked over by a car—I heard a Greek horn and a Greek shout—and that was when I saw the others, including Jamal, on the other side of the street, laughing. Holding their stomachs. They were laughing so hard, they could hardly stand. I swear that was the first and only time I've ever been inside a brothel.

I stayed in Athens until the middle of September. One day I shook Jamal's hand and got on a train for Corinth. It was rumored that the police in Patras were really bad, that some boys had come back with broken legs or broken arms or worse, and that, even though the journey to Italy was shorter from there, it was unpleasant and unhygienic, and you had to share it with the mice. I have a phobia of mice. Corinth, on the other hand, wasn't so bad, from what I'd heard. I found a Greek trafficker who hid people in lorries. The danger with lorries is that you're never sure where you're going to end up. You might think you're going to Italy and instead you find yourself in Germany, or if things work out really badly you might even end up back in Turkey. The trafficker asked me for four hundred and fifty euros, but I'd left the money for him in Athens, with Jamal.

I can't give it to you now, I said. When I get to Europe I'll call my friend and he can bring it to you. That or nothing.

All right, he said.

The thing to do in Corinth is go to the port, find a lorry and hide in the trailer, with the merchandise, or between the wheels. Over the next few weeks I hid several times, sometimes in quite dangerous places, but the inspectors always found me. The inspectors in Corinth are wily, and clued up to what goes on. They come in with their torches and they even look inside the boxes or sacks or go under the trailers and inspect every nook and cranny, which is what they're paid for, and I think a lot of them deserve every last cent of their salary. If they catch you, they don't arrest you, they just grab you by your jacket and chase you away. Sometimes with dogs.

So, after a while, I got fed up with these traffickers who couldn't organize anything and decided to do it myself. Jamal would hold the money for me.

I moved to the beach (you can sleep well on the beach, and take a shower). I joined a group of Afghans who were also dreaming of leaving, and it became like a kind of game. Every now and again, three or four of us would go to the port and try to get on a lorry. Some days when the weather was nice, and we were in a good mood, we even tried ten or eleven times, in a single day I mean. I managed it once, but the lorry—I told you this could happen—instead of embarking on a ship drove straight out of the port. I had no idea where it was going. I started to beat on the bodywork, from inside the trailer, and when we were about twenty or thirty minutes from the city the driver must have heard me. He stopped, got out and opened up. With a wrench in his hand. Although, when he saw that I was young (I think that was the reason), he didn't hit me. He screamed a few insults at me, which was only fair, and chased me away.

One evening, with a lovely sunset over the sea, I said to the boys on the beach, Let's go and try.

At the entrance to the port there were three containers one on top of the other, like a three-story building. I climbed to the top and, making myself as small as possible, squeezed in through a little hole. Suddenly, a machine hooked the building. I held my breath. The building was moved into the ship. One hour later, the freighter closed its hatches. I was very happy, I swear. I was really bursting with joy. I'd have liked to shout, but now wasn't the time. And besides, it was quite dark and I didn't know where I was going, and I didn't have anything to eat or drink, so I immediately calmed down and realized that before I could say that I'd made it, I had to see how it was going to end.

I stayed there for three days, shut up inside the belly of the ship. There were weird noises, all kinds of rumbling and roaring. Then the ship stopped. I heard the noise of the anchor dropping, which is a noise that's easy to recognize. Where am I? I wondered.

Italy

mustn't get up yet. I mustn't move. Keep still, breathe, wait. Be patient. Patience can save your life.

Once it had left the port—fifteen minutes had passed, I'd say, anyway less than half an hour—the lorry slowed down and entered a yard, a yard crammed full of other lorries and machines and trailers. My friends in Greece had advised me not to get out straightaway, but to wait until the lorry had traveled deep inside the country (whichever country it was), as far away from any border as possible, and then to take advantage of the driver stopping, at a motorway café for example, to slip out. I stayed there, all huddled up, calmly waiting for the lorry to set off again. I went over what I should do, so that I could be quick and accurate when the time came: jump to the ground, land on the tips of my toes, roll over if necessary to soften the blow, look for a way out, then run, don't turn around, just run.

But the lorry didn't set off again. Instead, I felt something like an earthquake. I leaned out. A huge crane had hooked the container I was in. I got really scared. What's going to happen? I thought. What if I end up in a metal crusher? I had to get out straightaway, I told myself, and jumped down.

Three men were working around the crane. I landed like a sack of potatoes (despite my mental rehearsals a bit earlier), because my legs were like wood and couldn't cushion the fall. As I landed, I let out a scream. And it may have been because of the scream, or because of the fact that they weren't expecting to see an Afghan fall out of the sky, but those three men were really scared, and even a guard dog that was there took fright and ran away. I'd fallen on concrete, but I couldn't let myself be distracted by the pain. Immediately looking for a way out, I noticed that part of the perimeter wall dividing the yard from the street had collapsed. I ran in that direction, on all fours, like a little animal: I couldn't stay on my feet. I thought the three men would follow me, instead of which one of them started shouting in English, Go, go, and pointing toward the main road. Nobody tried to stop me.

———

The first road sign I saw was a blue one.
On it was the word *Venice*.

I walked for a long time, along a road where there wasn't much traffic. Suddenly, I saw two figures in the distance, coming quickly toward me. As they got closer, I realized they were riding bicycles. When they saw me, they slowed down and stopped, probably because of my filthy clothes, or my filthy hair, or my face. They asked me if I was all right, if I needed anything, which I really appreciated. We spoke in English, as best we could, and when the first one said he was French I said, Zidane. Then, when the second one said he was Brazilian, I said, Ronaldinho. That was all I knew about their countries, and I wanted them to know how much I liked them. They asked me where I was from. Afghanistan, I said. They said, Taliban, Taliban. That was all they knew about my country.

One of them—the Brazilian, I think—gave me twenty euros. They indicated the direction of the nearest town, which was Mestre. I waved goodbye to them and started walking again, and walked until I found a bus stop. There were two or three people waiting, among them a very young boy. I went up to him and said in English, Train station?

Now I don't know who that boy was, maybe he was an angel, but he really helped me a lot. He told me to get on the bus with him. When we arrived in Venice, at Piazzale Roma, he bought me a roll because I must have looked as if I was hungry, then he took me to a church where he collected some new clothes for me and where I was able to wash, so that I didn't disgust people.

I may be stating the obvious, but isn't Venice beautiful? Everything on water. My God, I thought, I'm in paradise. Maybe all Italy is like this. In the meantime I kept saying to that boy, *Rome, Rome*, until he realized that I wanted to go to Rome. He went with me to the station and even bought me a ticket. Maybe he was related to the old Greek lady, I thought. In my opinion, kindness like that only gets handed on by example.

I had no idea how far it was from Venice to Rome or how long it would take me to get there. I didn't want to miss my stop, because then I'd be lost, so not surprisingly I was worried. I knew what I had to do when I got to Rome: I had the instructions memorized. I had to leave the central station and look for a number 175 bus in the square. Even in Greece we all knew that.

On the seat facing me was a fat gentleman who immediately opened his laptop to work. Every time we stopped at a station, or even if the train only slowed down, I leaned forward and said, *Please Rome, please Rome.* But there must have been a serious problem of communication between us, because whenever I said, *Please Rome, please Rome*, he would reply, *No rum, no rum*, because I pronounced *Rome* as *rum*.

After a while, after all this asking *Please Rome, please Rome*, the fat man started shouting angrily, *No rum. No. Enough.* He was really furious. He got up and walked away. I was afraid he was going to call the police. Instead of which he came back a few minutes later with a can of Coca-Cola and slammed it down in front of me and said, *No rum. Coca-Cola. No rum. Drink. Drink.*

I wasn't sure what had just happened, but you should never refuse a Coca-Cola, so I opened the can and drank and it struck me that the guy was really strange, first getting angry and then treating me to a Coke. Don't you agree? So, when we came to the next station—I was still sipping my Coca-Cola—I leaned over, innocently, and said, *Please Rome, please Rome.* At last, he understood. He said, *Rome.* Not *rum. Rome.*

I nodded.

Using hand gestures, he told me he was going to Rome, too, and that the central station—Termini, he called it—was his stop, and that I didn't have to worry, because it was the last stop. So at Rome we got off together. On the platform he shook my hand and said, *Bye bye*, and I replied, *Bye bye*, and we parted.

The square in front of the station was packed with cars, people and buses. I went around all the yellow bus stops until I found number 175. I knew I had to get off at the last stop.

It was dark by the time I got to Ostiense. There were lots of people there, the kind you call tramps and I call poor people, but no Afghans. Then I saw a long line of people against a wall, and there were Afghans among them. I joined the queue. They told me they were waiting to eat, and that the food was distributed by the monks from a monastery, and that if you asked them they also gave you blankets and cardboard boxes to bed down in.

Are you hungry? one of the monks asked when it was my turn.

I guessed what he was asking me, and I nodded. They gave me two rolls and two apples, nothing else.

How do you choose a place to settle, Enaiat? How can you tell one from another?

You recognize it because you don't feel like leaving. Not because it's perfect, obviously. There aren't any perfect places. But there are places where at least no one tries to hurt you.

If you hadn't stayed in Italy, where would you have gone?

I don't know. Paris, maybe.

And is there a place like Ostiense in Paris?

Yes, I think there's a bridge where you can go. I can't remember which bridge, but I know you get there by bus. I even used to know the number of the bus. Now, fortunately, I've forgotten it.

I had two hundred euros in my pocket, my savings from Greece. I had to decide in a hurry what to do, because if I needed to buy a ticket or something like that, I couldn't expect that money to grow in my pocket like a plant, could I? There are moments when you give the future a strange name, and at that moment the name of my future was Payam.

As I mentioned before, I knew Payam was in Italy, but not exactly where, and as a lot of people live in Italy, I had to get cracking if I wanted to find him. So I started looking for him, mentioning his name to everyone, and after all that mentioning of his name, one day I met someone who told me he had a friend who was in England now and who might have talked to him about a boy called Payam who he'd met in a reception center in Crotone, in Calabria. Of course, it could have been another Payam. There's no copyright on names.

We went to a call shop and phoned this friend in London, who had found work in a bar.

I have a mobile number if you want it, he said.

Of course, I replied. Do you know where he lives?

In Turin.

I wrote down the mobile number on a piece of paper and dialed it without even leaving the booth.

Hello?

Yes. Hello. I'd like to talk to Payam.

Payam speaking. Who's that?

Enaiatollah Akbari. From Nava.

Silence.

Hello? I said.

Yes, I can hear you.

This is Enaiatollah Akbari. From Nava.

Silence.

Is that you, Payam?

Yes, this is Payam. Are you really Enaiatollah? Where are you calling from?

Rome.

That's not possible.

Why not?

What are you doing in Italy?

What are *you* doing in Italy?

Payam really couldn't believe it was me. He asked me trick questions about our village and my relatives and his. I answered everything correctly. In the end he said, What are you planning to do?

I don't know.

Then come to Turin.

We said goodbye and I went to Termini station to catch the train. On that occasion, I remember, I learned my first word of Italian. I got an Afghan to go with me, someone who had been in Italy for a while and spoke the language quite well, to buy the ticket and make sure I got on the right train. He came into the carriage with me, looked around, chose a kind-looking lady and spoke to her. This boy has to get off in Turin, he said. The word he used was *scendere*. As it happens, *shin* is an Iranian word meaning "stone." It stuck in my mind, and I found I could get my mouth around the words *shindere* Turin, *shindere* Turin. If I said that, I'd avoid mix-ups, like when I'd come to Rome.

During the journey the lady asked me if I had the number of someone who could come and pick me up from Porta Nuova station. I gave her Payam's number and she called him to make arrangements. She told him what time we'd be arriving and where. Everything went well. In Turin, surrounded by trolleys and bags and a party of children coming back from a trip, Payam and I barely recognized each other. We hadn't seen each other since I was nine (maybe) and now I was fifteen (maybe) and he was two or three years older than me. Our language sounded strange to us the way it never had when we were children.

———

It was Payam who went with me to the Office for Foreign Minors, without even giving me time to get used to the shapes of the houses or the coolness of the air (it was the middle of September). He had immediately asked me—I still felt the warmth of his embrace on my chest— what my intentions were, because I couldn't stay unde- cided for too long: indecisiveness wasn't healthy for someone who didn't have asylum. He knew this because, when he arrived, he didn't have asylum, but he was lucky and some people had helped him. I looked outside the window of the café we'd gone into for a cappuccino—I know a place where they make the best cappuccinos in the city, he'd said—and I thought of the boy in Venice and the lady on the train to Turin. I'd liked both of them so much, they made me want to live in the same country where they lived. If all Italians are like that, I thought, then this might be a place where I could settle. To tell the truth, I was tired. Tired of traveling all the time. So I said to Payam, I want to stay in Italy. And he said, All right. He smiled, paid for the cappuccino, waved to the barman, who he seemed to know, and we set off on foot for the Office for Foreign Minors.

The sun was setting and there was a strong wind sweeping the streets. By the time we got there it was late and the office was closing. Payam spoke on my behalf, and when the lady told him there wasn't a place for me in any of the social housing, and that for a week I'd have to fend for myself, he asked the lady to wait a moment, turned and repeated every word to me. I shrugged my shoulders. We thanked her and left.

He was living in social housing and couldn't put me up.

I can sleep in a park, I said.

I don't want you to sleep in a park, Enaiat. I have a friend in a village just outside Turin, I'll ask him to put you up. So Payam called this friend of his, who immediately agreed. We went to the bus station together and Payam told me I shouldn't get off until I saw someone stick their head in and tell me to follow him. That's what I did. After an hour's journey, at one of the stops, an Afghan boy put his head in at the door and made a sign to me with his hand that I'd arrived.

I went to the Afghan boy's place but after three days—I'm not sure what had happened—it turned out he wasn't happy about it, he was sorry and all that, but he couldn't put me up anymore. He said I was an illegal, even though I'd gone to the Office for Foreign Minors of my own free will, and if the police found me in his house there was a risk he would lose his papers.

As was only right, I told him not to worry, I didn't want to cause him any trouble. I've slept in parks for so long, I said, that a few more nights certainly won't harm me.

But when Payam found out, he again said, No, I don't want you to sleep in the park. Let me call a social worker.

The person he called was an Italian woman named Danila who had apparently, like us, tried to talk to the Office for Foreign Minors, but it really did seem that there wasn't even a broom cupboard that had room for me, so she—Danila—had said to Payam, Bring him to my house.

When Payam and I met, he said, There's a family that are going to put you up.

A family? I said. What do you mean, *a family*?

A father, a mother and children, that's what.

I don't want to go to a family.

Why?

I don't know how to behave. I'm not going there.

Why? How should you behave? You just have to be nice.

I'm sure I'll be a nuisance to them.

No. I assure you. I know them well.

Payam kept insisting I should accept Danila's offer until he was hoarse, as anyone would do with a person he likes and feels responsible for. He wouldn't even hear about leaving me alone at night, knowing I'd be sleeping on a bench. So in the end I gave in. More for his sake than mine.

The family lived outside Turin, in an isolated house beyond the hills. Getting out of the car—Danila had come to pick us up from the bus stop—I was greeted by three dogs, and as dogs are probably my favorite animals, I thought, This doesn't look too bad at all.

The father was called Marco, and even though he's a father, I can call him by his name, not like my father, who I have only called Father. And the children, Matteo and Francesco, I feel up to saying their names too. They aren't names that cause me pain.

As soon as we entered the house they gave me these big slippers, shaped like rabbits, with ears and a nose and everything—maybe they did it as a joke—and after washing our hands we had dinner at the table, with forks and knives and glasses and napkins and all that, and I was so afraid of making a fool of myself that I copied every single gesture they made. I remember there was also an old woman with them at dinner that evening. She sat stiffly, with her wrists resting on the table, and so I did the same: I stiffened my back and placed my wrists on the table, and seeing that she wiped her mouth after every bite, I wiped my mouth after every bite, too. I remember that Danila had made a starter, a first course, and a second course. My God, I remember thinking, these people eat so much.

After dinner they showed me a room. There was a bed in the room, just one, and it was all mine. Danila came up, bringing me pajamas. Here you are, she said. But I didn't know what pajamas were. I was used to sleeping in my clothes. I took off my socks and put them under the bed, and when Danila gave me those pajamas, I put them under the bed, too. Marco brought me a towel and a bathrobe. Matteo wanted to play me some of his favorite CDs. Francesco had dressed as an Indian—an American Indian—and called me to see his toys. They were all trying to tell me things, but I didn't understand a word.

When I woke up in the morning, Danila and Marco had gone to work and the only other person in the house was Francesco, who was about to leave for school. I found out later that he was worried about my presence, and was wondering, What's this guy up to? At the same time, I was afraid to leave my room, and only went down (my room was in the attic) when Francesco called to me from the bottom of the stairs to say that, if I wanted, breakfast was ready. And it was true. On the table in the kitchen were biscuits and fresh orange juice. Fantastic. That whole day was fantastic. The next few days were fantastic. I would happily have stayed there forever. Because when you're welcomed by people who treat you well—but in a natural way, without being intrusive—then you just want to go on being welcomed. Don't you agree?

The one problem was language, but when I realized that Danila and Marco liked to hear me tell my story, I started talking and talking and talking, in English and in Afghan, with my mouth and with my hands, with my eyes and with objects. Do they understand or not? I asked myself. Be patient, I answered myself, and carried on talking.

Until the day when a bed became free in a hostel for migrants.

I went there by myself, on foot.

There'll be an Iranian lady there who can act as your interpreter, they said.

Good. Thanks.

It's a place where you can have a quiet life, they said.

Good. Thanks.

Do you want to know anything else?

Study. Work.

Just go there first, then we'll see.

Good. Thanks.

But there wasn't any Iranian lady. They'd told me I could have a quiet life there, which was true, I could. But the place itself wasn't quiet at all. There was constant shouting and quarreling. And besides, it was more like a prison than a home. As soon as I arrived, they confiscated my belt and wallet with the little money I had. The doors were closed from the outside, and sealed. You couldn't go out (and you can imagine how accustomed I was to freedom, after all those years spent going all over the place by myself). I mean, I appreciated everything, it was still a clean, warm place, and there was pasta and things like that for dinner, but I wanted to work or study—preferably study—instead of which two months went by, under me, like water flowing under a transparent sheet of glass, and for two months I didn't do anything, didn't even speak, because I still didn't know the language, although I tried to learn it from the books I'd been given by Marco and Danila. The only distractions were watching television, in silence, and sleeping and eating. In silence.

Doing nothing wasn't what I'd planned, and I couldn't receive visits, not even from the family who'd looked after me. But after two months Danila and Marco started to worry and arranged for a youth worker named Sergio, who wasn't only a youth worker but also a friend of theirs and someone who was known to the home, to pick me up on Saturday afternoons and take me to spend some of my free time (and I had plenty of that) with the boys from a youth group.

Sergio came to fetch me, and that first Saturday was a wonderful day. When I got to the youth group, I found Payam there. He took me by the hand and introduced me to everyone. Danila was also there. So I got a chance to talk to Danila, and tell her, thank you thank you, but I wasn't really very happy in that place, for these reasons, that I hadn't come all this way just to eat, sleep and watch television. I wanted to study and work. At that point Danila made a face like someone who's thinking about something, and the thing they're thinking about is important, but at that moment, even though it seemed as if she had something to say to me, she didn't say anything. The following week, though, when I went back to the youth group, she came up to me, took me aside and in a low voice, as if the words weighed on her, asked me if I'd like to go and stay with them, because they wanted to do something to help me, and they had plenty of room, as I'd seen, and if I liked that room they could give it to me. Not only would I like to, I replied, but it was a really fantastic idea.

So Danila and Marco sent off the request. A few days later, the time it took to get through the paperwork, they came and fetched me from the home. They told me I was being fostered. They explained what that meant, that I had a house and a family, three dogs, my own room, and even a wardrobe where I could put my clothes. They explained that I was the first child they had fostered, but they could see I was the right one.

The thing they didn't need to explain, because I already knew, was that we were going to get on well with each other.

That's how it started. What I'd call my new life. Or at least, the first step. Because now that I'd been welcomed in the house of Marco and Danila, I had to try and stay there, and staying there meant not getting myself expelled from Italy, and not getting myself expelled from Italy meant being recognized as a political refugee and granted asylum.

The first problem was the language. I spoke very little Italian. Everyone made an effort to help me. I could barely read the Latin alphabet, and was always confusing zero with the letter *O*. Even the pronunciation was difficult.

It might be better if you did some courses, said Danila.

School? I asked.

School, she said.

I gave her a thumbs-up sign to let her know how pleased I was. I remembered the school in Quetta, the one where I went to hear the children play. In a fit of euphoria, I chose three courses, because I was afraid that one wasn't enough. I would leave with Danila in the morning, when she went to work, at eight, then walk around until half past nine, when it was time for my first class at the Parini Adult Education Center, which is something they have in Turin, and also in other cities, too, at least I think so. Then I left, went to another school, attended my second class, came out again, went to the youth group, attended the Italian classes there in the afternoon, and at that point, happy and exhausted, returned home. This went on for six months. In the meantime my friend Payam continued acting as my interpreter when I couldn't manage by myself, for example at home, when someone had to tell me something and I didn't understand, they'd phone him and he'd translate. Sometimes Danila even called him to find out what I wanted for dinner, even though I really didn't mind what I ate as long as it was something that filled my belly.

In June I took the middle school exam (even though the teachers at the Parini Center didn't want me to, they said it was too early, but that was because of that old question of time, which isn't the same everywhere in the world).

In September I enrolled in upper school, where I immediately cut a sorry figure. Or rather, I think I did, because I sometimes don't notice when something funny or strange happens, because if I *did* notice, I would avoid it happening, would avoid being made to feel a fool, and so on. Once the health education teacher called me to the blackboard and asked me to write things, I can't remember what, something to do with chemistry, or with sums, but instead of numbers there were letters or something like that. I said I didn't understand it at all. She explained it to me, but I said again that I didn't understand, not even her explanation.

What school have you been to? she asked.

I said I hadn't gone to school.

What? she said.

I said I'd done six months of Italian classes and then the high school exam as an external student and that was it.

What about before that? she asked.

I said I hadn't done anything before that. Yes, I'd gone to school in Afghanistan, in my little village, with my teacher who wasn't alive anymore, but that was it.

She got very upset. She went to the principal to complain and for a moment I was afraid I'd be thrown out of the school, which would have been a tragedy for me, because school was the one thing that interested me. Fortunately, another teacher intervened. She was patient, she said, we would take things one step at a time, health education and psychology could wait, and we'd give priority to the other subjects. So, as there was a boy in my school who was a bit handicapped, and he had special support, while I didn't, for a few months I took advantage of the opportunity and during the health education and psychology periods I left the class and studied with him.

Language, Enaiat. As you're talking and telling me your story, I keep thinking you're not using the language you learned from your mother. At evening classes, right now, you're studying history, science, math, geography, and you're studying these subjects in a language that isn't the one you learned from your mother. The names of the food you eat aren't in the language you learned from your mother. You joke with your friends in a language you didn't learn from your mother. You'll become a man in a language you didn't learn from your mother. You bought your first car in a language you didn't learn from your mother. When you're tired, you rest in a language you didn't learn from your mother. When you laugh, you laugh in a language you didn't learn from your mother. When you dream, I don't know in what language you dream. But I know, Enaiat, that you'll fall in love in a language you didn't learn from your mother.

I remember I didn't get on too well with my classmates during the first year, because I really liked being at school. For me it was a privilege. I studied a lot and if I got a bad mark I immediately went to the teacher to say I wanted to catch up, and that was something that bothered the others a lot. Even those who were younger than me said I was a swot.

Then things started getting better. I made friends. I learned a lot of things that forced me to look at life with different eyes, like when you put on a pair of sunglasses with tinted lenses. When I studied health education, I was surprised by what they told me, because when I compared it to my past, to the conditions I'd lived in, the food I'd eaten, and so on, I wondered how it was possible that I was still in one piece.

I was at the end of my second year when a letter came to the house saying that I had to go to Rome to meet the commission that would decide if I could be granted asylum as a political refugee. I'd been expecting that letter. I'd been expecting it because I'd met an Afghan boy at the Parini Center who'd arrived in Italy just before me and whose story was very similar to mine. So everything that happened to him tended to happen to me, too, like being summoned because of his papers and things like that. He'd received the letter a few months earlier, had gone to Rome, had met the commission and the outcome had been that he wasn't recognized as a political refugee. I remember his desperation when he came back and told me. I couldn't understand it. Why hadn't they granted him asylum? If they hadn't granted him asylum, they wouldn't grant me asylum. I remember that he put his head in his hands, this friend of mine, and wept, but without tears, wept with his voice and his shoulders, and said, Now where can I go?

One day I left on a train with Marco and Danila and traveled the same route I'd taken to get from Rome to Turin but in the opposite direction. We presented ourselves punctually in this building in an area the name of which I forget. We waited a short while, then they called my name, which echoed down the corridor. Marco and Danila stayed there. I went in.

Sit down, they said.

I sat down.

This is your interpreter, they said, indicating a boy next to the door.

I said I preferred to do without. Thank you.

So you speak Italian well, they said.

I replied that yes, I spoke it quite well. But that wasn't the only reason I didn't want an interpreter. If you speak directly to people you convey emotions more intensely. Even if you stumble over your words and don't get the intonation right, the message you get across is closer to what you have in your head, compared with what an interpreter could repeat—don't you think so?—because emotions can't come from the mouth of an interpreter, only words, and words are just a shell. We chatted for forty-five minutes. I told them everything. I told them about Nava, about my father and mother, about the journey, about how, when I slept in Marco and Danila's house in Turin, my nights would be disturbed by nightmares, a bit like the wind disturbing the sea between Turkey and Greece, and in those nightmares I was running away from something and, in running, I often fell out of bed, or else I would get up, tear off the blanket, wrap it around my shoulders, go downstairs, open the door of the yard and go and sleep in the car, all without realizing it, or else I would neatly fold my clothes on one side, and lie down in the bathroom, in a corner. I told them I always sought out the corners to sleep in. I was a sleepwalker. I told them all this, and after a while the commissioner said that he couldn't understand why I wanted political asylum because in Afghanistan the situation wasn't so dangerous for Afghans, when you came down to it, and I would be perfectly all right if I could be in my own home.

Then I took out a newspaper. It was a daily paper from a few days earlier. I pointed to an article.

The headline was *Afghanistan: Taliban boy cuts spy's throat.*

The article was about a young boy without a name who'd been filmed cutting the throat of a prisoner and crying *Allah Akbar*. The sequence had been broadcast by the Taliban as propaganda in the border areas of Pakistan. In the video you saw the prisoner, an Afghan man, confess his guilt in front of a group of militants, many of them teenagers. Then they showed the executioner, a very young boy wearing a combat jacket a few sizes too big for him. He's an American spy, the boy said straight to the camera. He was carrying a large knife. People like him deserve to die, he said. At that point a Taliban lifted the condemned man's beard and they all cried *Allah Akbar, Allah Akbar, God is great*, and the little boy sank the knife into the man's throat.

I pointed at the article and said, I could have ended up like that.

A few days later, I heard I'd been granted asylum.

Three years passed. It was during my third year at upper school that I thought the moment had come to try and contact my mother. I could have looked for her before, but it was only after obtaining asylum, only after I'd acquired the necessary tranquillity, that I started thinking again about her and my brother and sister. For a long time I had wiped them from my mind. Not out of spite or anything, but because before coming to terms with other people you have to come to terms with yourself. How can you give love if you don't love your own life? When I realized that I really liked it in Italy, I called one of my Afghan friends in Qom, whose father was in Pakistan, in Quetta, and asked him if he thought it was possible for his father to try and get in touch with my family in Afghanistan.

If your father managed to find my mother, brother and sister, I said, I could pay him for his trouble and also let him have enough money to take all of them with him to Quetta. I told him where they lived and so on. He (my friend in Iran) said, It'll be complicated for me to explain all these things. I'll give you the telephone number of my uncle and father. Call them in Pakistan and you do it. All right?

So I called his father and he was very kind. He said not to think about the money. He said that if they were in Afghanistan, in that little valley, and they didn't know if I was alive or dead, just as I didn't know if they were alive or dead, then he considered finding them a duty.

I replied that I'd pay for the journey and expenses anyway, even if he did consider it a duty, because a sense of duty is a good thing, but money's important, too. Plus, it could be a dangerous journey. Through a war zone.

Time passed. I'd almost given up hope. Then, one evening, I received a phone call. The hoarse voice of my friend's father greeted me: he sounded very close. He told me it had been difficult to find them, because they'd left Nava and moved to a village on the other side of the valley, but that in the end he'd succeeded, and that when he'd told my mother that I'd been the one to ask for them to move to Quetta, she hadn't believed it, and didn't want to leave. He'd had to work hard to convince her to come with him, but she had.

Then he said, Wait. He wanted to give someone the phone. And my eyes filled with tears, because I already knew who that someone was.

Mother, I said.

There was no reply at the other end.

Mother, I repeated.

All I could hear through the receiver was breathing, soft and moist and slightly sharp. I realized that she, too, was crying. We were talking to each other for the first time in eight years, and that sharpness and those sighs were all that a son and a mother can say to each other, after all that time. We continued like that, both silent, until we were cut off.

That was when I knew she was still alive, and maybe it was also then that I realized, for the first time, that I was, too.

I'm not quite sure how. But I was.

Enaiatollah finished telling his story soon after turning twenty-one (maybe). The date of his birthday has been decided by the authorities: it is September 1, 1989. His mother is living in Pakistan and he hopes to see her soon. He has recently discovered that there really are crocodiles in the sea.

Fabio Geda is an Italian novelist who works with children who are under duress. He writes for several Italian magazines and newspapers and teaches creative writing at Scuola Holden, the Italian school of storytelling in Turin. This is his first book to be translated into English.

Enaiatollah Akbari graduated from high school in the spring of 2011 and plans to attend university in Italy while continuing to support his mother and siblings, who are now living in Pakistan. He dreams of having the chance to return one day to a democratic and peaceful Afghanistan.

Howard Curtis is a London-based translator of Italian and French texts, for which he has won numerous awards, including the John Florio Prize for Italian Translation. He was short-listed for the 2010 Independent Foreign Fiction Prize.

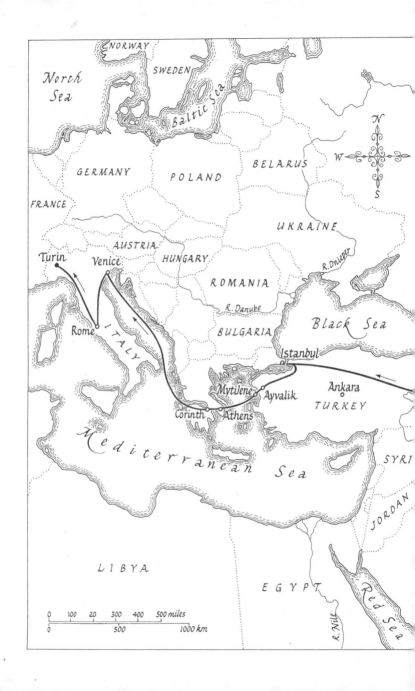